BAD MOONLIGHT . . . SHINING DOWN ON ME

"Go!" Danielle whispered to herself.

She started to run.

The weeds whipped at her legs and dress, but she didn't slow down.

She couldn't slow down.

The moonlight. Something about the moonlight.

A shape loomed in front of her. A wall. Big stones with wrought-iron bars sunk into the top. The wall stood at least five feet high.

Stop, Danielle thought. *Stop!*

She couldn't stop.

She ran at the stone wall. She felt the muscles in her legs tighten and bunch like springs.

And then, she leaped. Off the ground. Soaring into the air. Over the wall. She landed on all fours.

How did I do that?

Books by R. L. Stine

Available from ARCHWAY Paperbacks

FEAR STREET®
SUPER CHILLER
R·L·STINE

Bad Moonlight

A Parachute Press Book

AN ARCHWAY PAPERBACK
Published by POCKET BOOKS
New York   London   Toronto   Sydney   Tokyo   Singapore

AN ARCHWAY PAPERBACK *Original*

An Archway Paperback published by
POCKET BOOKS, a division of Simon & Schuster Inc.
1230 Avenue of the Americas, New York, NY 10020

ISBN: 0-671-89424-2

First Archway Paperback printing June 1995

10 9 8 7 6 5 4 3 2 1

Cover art by David Jarvis

Printed in the U.S.A.

IL 7+

Bad Moonlight

Prologue

A half-moon shimmered hazily in the supermarket window, a pale reflection of the bright moon high in the night sky. The automatic door buzzed as Danielle Verona stepped into the glare of fluorescent light inside the store.

She shivered and rubbed her bare arms. The store air conditioner must be turned up to superfreeze, she thought. Danielle wore a sleeveless blue midriff shirt, white short-shorts, and sandals. I'd better stay away from the frozen foods section, she decided.

She caught a glimpse of her reflection in a silvery display case. Her round, dark eyes stared back at her. She pushed back her straight brown hair, streaked with blond.

I'm so thin and shapeless, Danielle thought, frowning at herself. I look twelve instead of eighteen.

A sudden, sharp pain in her back made her spin away from her reflection. "Cliff—stop it!" she snapped. "Do you have to use your head as a weapon?"

Her ten-year-old brother grinned at her. Head-butting was his new hobby.

"Stop running into me like that. I'm going to be black and blue!" Danielle declared angrily.

"You're a wimp," Cliff said. "I hardly touched you."

"Give your sister a break," Aunt Margaret scolded, pushing the grocery cart up to them. "Danielle just got home, Cliff. She's tired. She doesn't need you giving her a hard time."

"Yes, she does," Cliff insisted, still grinning. He was built more like their father—short and chubby, with a babyish round face. His straw-colored hair was shaved short on the sides, brushed back long on top.

"Here—you take the cart," Aunt Margaret said sharply. She shoved it toward Cliff. "Why do I always get one with a wheel that sticks?"

Cliff grabbed the handle of the grocery cart and zoomed away. He ran full-speed down the aisle, the cart zigzagging wildly from side to side.

"Cliff—look out!" Aunt Margaret shouted. She turned to Danielle. "He's so excited to see you," she confided softly.

Danielle rolled her eyes. "He sure has a strange way of showing it!"

2

They watched Cliff whirl the cart around and come clattering back toward them. "He's not used to your being away for two weeks," Aunt Margaret said. "But I'm so glad it's working out for you, dear."

She was a small but sturdy woman. Sharp-featured. Beaklike nose. Pointed chin. With her bleached red hair, steely blue eyes, and heavy red lipstick, Danielle's aunt looked tough. Hard.

When Danielle's parents had died almost three years before, Aunt Margaret had moved across the country to take care of her and Cliff. Danielle hadn't seen her aunt in years, and she'd been unsure about how they'd get along. But Aunt Margaret turned out to be a wonderful, loving mother to Cliff and Danielle.

She put a hand on Danielle's shoulder. "You're so cold!"

Danielle shrugged. "I didn't exactly dress for the arctic!"

They started walking slowly down the first aisle. Vegetables on one side, fruit on the other. At the end of the aisle a young man in a white apron was spraying the lettuces with a hose, making them glisten.

"Did you think of a name for the band?" Aunt Margaret asked, dropping a bag of carrots into the cart.

"Yuck! Carrots!" Cliff complained.

"Not yet," Danielle told her aunt. "Caroline wanted to call us the Musically Challenged. We all thought that was pretty funny. But Billy thought it was too negative."

"Billy is the leader?" Aunt Margaret asked, tearing

off a plastic bag. She bent to select some baking potatoes from a basket on the floor.

"Your band reeks," Cliff commented. He tapped Aunt Margaret's shoulder. "Can we buy candy?"

"No," Aunt Margaret replied quickly. Then she changed her mind. She stood up and dropped the potatoes into the cart. "Okay. Go, Cliff. Go pick out some candy. I'll take the cart."

"All right!" he cried happily. He deliberately bumped Danielle hard, nearly knocking her over, as he sped off down the aisle.

"What a character," Aunt Margaret muttered. She turned to Danielle, her tiny eyes studying her niece. "You look tired."

Danielle sighed. "Two weeks on the road. Bumping along in the van. Playing tiny music clubs."

"I'm so glad you're doing it," her aunt said. "I'm glad you decided to try the band instead of going straight to college. You need a year to be out on your own, to travel around and have some fun before going back to school."

"Well, I *am* having fun," Danielle told her. "And Caroline and I have become really close friends."

"Caroline is the piano player?" Aunt Margaret asked.

"Electronic keyboard. And she sings backup," Danielle replied. "Making a new friend has been really nice. And the band has been getting pretty good crowds. But I sure do miss having home-cooked meals. All week I was thinking, if I have to choke down one more greasy hamburger . . ."

4

Aunt Margaret chuckled. She had a quiet, dry laugh that sounded more like a cough. "Well, tonight is your choice night," she said. "You decide. I'll make anything you want for our special late dinner."

"Hmmmm . . ." Danielle narrowed her dark eyes, thinking hard. "What do I want?" She smiled. "Oh. I know. That special chicken you make. You know. With the pineapples. Sort of oriental?"

"Okay. You've got it," Aunt Margaret replied.

"And mashed potatoes," Danielle added. "I've been thinking a lot about your mashed potatoes."

"You're a weird child," Aunt Margaret teased. "But mashed potatoes it is." She wandered off down the aisle, struggling to push the three-wheeled cart.

Danielle shivered. Why do they keep it so cold in here? she wondered. Do people buy more food when they're half-frozen?

She made her way down the back aisle, searching for Cliff. In the soaps and detergents aisle, she thought she saw a friend from Shadyside High. She hurried up to him and was about to call out—when he turned around. A stranger.

Danielle moved past him, avoiding his glance.

The aisles blended together. The harsh fluorescent light from above gave everything a green tinge. The shelves of jars and cans, the displays, the shoppers all seemed too bright, too sharply focused. Not real.

She walked on. The harsh light flashed in her eyes. She shivered again. The frigid air made goosebumps rise up and down her arms.

5

"Danielle—what are you *doing?*" Cliff's shrill voice broke through her thoughts.

"Huh?" She glanced down at the package in her hand.

A package of raw beef. From the butcher's shelf.

The package had been ripped open, Danielle saw. She was squeezing a hunk of raw, purple meat in one hand.

Her mouth was full. She swallowed the raw meat she had been chewing. It felt cold and slimy as it slid down her throat.

"Danielle—why are you eating that? What's *wrong* with you?" Cliff cried in alarm.

"I—I don't know!" Danielle stammered, feeling the cold red blood running down her chin.

PART ONE

SONGS

Chapter 1

OFF A CLIFF

"**J**oey—please slow down," Danielle pleaded.

The van bounced over a deep pothole in the highway. The bags and instruments strapped to the top thudded against the roof.

"I'll slow down if you'll come up here and sit on my lap," Joey declared.

Danielle could see his grin in the rearview mirror. "No way!" she told him. "Stop being such a jerk, Joey. We don't want to be pulled over again."

He let out a high-pitched laugh and jammed his foot down on the gas pedal. The van roared and shot forward, tossing Danielle back against the seat.

"Joey—!" Oh, what's the use, she thought unhappily. He thinks it's so cool to drive fast. He isn't going to change.

9

Joey let out a happy cry. His curly black hair fluttered behind his head in the rush of air through the open van window. Even though it was night, he drove with his sunglasses over his eyes.

Danielle sat between Caroline and Mary Beth in the second seat. "I give up. He's just impossible," she murmured to them.

"You girls must be jammed tight back there!" Joey shouted over the roar of the wind. "Come on. Who wants to sit on my lap?" Wheeling around a curve, he patted his leg.

They ignored him.

As always.

Headlights from an oncoming truck swept over the van. Danielle shielded her eyes. She bumped against Caroline as Joey swerved the van sharply to the right.

"Hey—watch it!" Caroline protested to Joey. She reached up and tugged his fluttering hair.

"Caroline, are you flirting with me?" he called back.

She let go of his hair. "For sure," she muttered sarcastically. "I only flirt with members of my own species!"

Danielle and Mary Beth laughed. Caroline had a quick mind and a sharp sense of humor.

Behind them in the backseat, Billy and Kit were asleep. Their heads bounced against the seatbacks as Joey stormed along the narrow highway. But the bouncing and jarring didn't wake them.

Danielle glanced back at the two guys.

Billy Dark was the manager of the band. At twenty-two he was the group's oldest member. Kit Kragen was two years younger than Billy. Kit was a roadie, the equipment manager. But he was so good looking, girls in the audience usually paid more attention to him than to the band members!

Far below the guardrail, dark farms and empty fields whirred by. The air from the van's open windows felt hot and damp.

"I've been thinking about names for us," Caroline said. "And I thought maybe—"

"That's all we ever think about," Mary Beth interrupted. She was a short, pretty girl, with straight, carrot-colored hair cut very short and intense green eyes.

Intense was the perfect word to describe Mary Beth, Danielle thought. Mary Beth took *everything* seriously. She was the band's drummer, and her playing was as precise and intense as her mind.

"I think we should call ourselves the Beatles and stop thinking about it," Caroline joked.

Danielle laughed. "Wasn't there already a group with that name?"

"And they did okay—didn't they?" Caroline replied. "So maybe the name will work for us!"

"Can't you guys ever be serious?" Dee Waters demanded, turning in the front passenger seat to face the other three girls. She wore her dark hair in tightly braided cornrows. Her long, amber earrings matched her almond-shaped eyes and complemented her brown skin.

Dee had been so quiet, Danielle had practically forgotten she was sitting up there. Caroline, Mary

Beth, and Danielle had been talking the entire trip. Dee had stared silently out the window, refusing to join in.

Will she ever be friendly to me? Danielle wondered.

Will Dee ever get over her resentment that she's not the band's lead singer anymore?

Danielle suddenly remembered her audition for the band. Caroline's family had an unfinished room above their garage. The band used it for rehearsals. Danielle had auditioned for them there.

She had been so nervous. She knew she had a good voice. And she knew she was a pretty good songwriter.

But would they like her?

When she arrived, they had all greeted her warmly. Billy had been especially kind. He introduced everyone, making little jokes about each one. "Watch out for Kit," Billy warned. "He bites."

Danielle's hands trembled as she opened her guitar case and prepared to sing one of her own songs for them.

"Everybody be nice to Danielle," Billy told the others as they sprawled around the small room. "She's going to be a famous songwriter some day."

The room was cluttered with amps and guitar cases and coils of cable. Joey, the sound guy, plugged her guitar into an amp for her. He flashed her a thumbs-up.

The others smiled and watched eagerly as Danielle sat down on a tall stool and tuned up.

They had all been so nice, so welcoming.

Everyone but Dee.

Dee had sat glumly against the wall with her arms crossed. Her unhappy expression never changed.

Even when Danielle finished her first song to applause and cheers, Dee didn't move. She stared at Danielle, a bitter expression on her face.

After her second song they made Danielle wait outside. It didn't take them long to make a decision about her. Billy came hurrying down the steps. "You're in!" he told her, wrapping her in a warm hug. "You and Dee will be lead singers. And we want to learn that second song you sang. It's really excellent!"

What a happy day that was.

If only Dee hadn't tried to spoil it. She had come up to Danielle in the driveway as Danielle started to her car. Dee whispered her words. But Danielle heard them very clearly.

"You don't belong in this band."

That's what Dee had said. Her whisper so cold. Like a chill wind.

"You don't belong in this band."

And then Dee turned, her eyes darting around, making sure none of the others had seen her. She strode quickly away, returning to the garage.

Danielle had tried to win her over ever since.

But Dee remained cold and unfriendly.

"I don't know why I stay with this band," Dee was saying, turning from the front seat. "I mean, no name? A band with no name? That's just pitiful."

"You stay because you're hot for *me!*" Joey chimed in. He took his right hand off the wheel and slid it around Dee's shoulder. "Admit it, babes."

"Get your hand off me," Dee warned playfully. She grabbed his wrist and started twisting it. "Unless you want to drive one-handed for the rest of your life!"

"Ooh!" Joey cried. "I love it when you come on to me like that!"

Dee let out a cry of disgust.

Joey returned his hand to the wheel. But he turned back to Danielle, Caroline, and Mary Beth. "I know what you should call the band!" he shouted, grinning.

"Joey—please!" Danielle pleaded. "Watch the road! We're on the edge of a cliff!"

"You should call it Joey's Groupies!" he declared. He tossed back his head, his long hair flying behind him, and started to utter a loud howl.

But the cry was cut short as the van slid out of control.

Danielle shrieked.

The tires squealed as Joey hit the brake.

Too late.

Danielle heard the crush of metal as the van crashed through the low metal guardrail.

She screamed again as the van sailed off the edge of the cliff.

14

Chapter 2

WHAT'S WRONG WITH ME?

*T*he van shot through the night sky. Far below, Danielle could see jagged rocks at the bottom of the cliff.

The rocks gleamed like knives in the moonlight.

Then the van's nose tilted down.

Danielle pitched forward violently in her seat. She screamed again as the van aimed straight for the gleaming moonlit rocks.

She felt a rough jolt, followed by the sickening crunch of metal. The van's front wheels struck the rocks.

Danielle's head snapped back. The windshield shattered. Glass flew into the van.

We're going to die, Danielle thought. We're all going to die!

"We're going to die!" she screamed aloud.

"Danielle!"

"No!" Danielle cried. She bent forward and covered her face with her hands. The van was flipping over. Tumbling through the air like a toy car.

In seconds we'll all be dead, Danielle thought. She squeezed her palms against her eyes and waited for the fatal impact.

A hand touched her shoulder. It felt warm and comforting. Long fingers gripped her tightly and gave her a gentle shake.

"Danielle!"

Caroline's voice.

Slowly Danielle looked up. Her friend's blue eyes were filled with concern. "Danielle, it's okay," Caroline murmured softly. "Everything's okay."

"But the van—" Danielle stopped. She could feel the van's rocking motion as it moved smoothly along the highway. She could hear the whine of the tires on the road. She raised her eyes to the windshield. Smooth, unbroken glass.

We didn't crash, she thought. It never happened. It was a fantasy. A violent, terrifying fantasy.

Danielle took a deep, shaky breath. Her heart was still beating wildly.

"What happened?" Caroline asked. "What was it, Danielle?"

"The van went off the cliff!" she gasped. "Joey howled, and then the van went out of control. I could see us crashing through the guardrail. I saw the windshield crack. I even felt it when we hit the rocks!"

"No wonder you screamed like that," Mary Beth said softly.

Danielle took another deep breath and glanced around. Billy and Kit were wide awake now. Staring at her. Dee was watching her, too, frowning.

Danielle turned away and met Joey's shade-covered eyes in the rearview mirror. Joey grinned, a little shame-faced. "Sorry about that, Danny," he told her. "I didn't mean to scare you."

"You *should* be sorry," Dee snapped. "We're lucky you *didn't* drive us off the cliff."

Joey shrugged. "Hey, I said I was sorry. Anyway, blame the moon." He chuckled and pointed out the window. "Almost full tonight, see? The moon always makes me a little wild."

Danielle glanced out the window at the night sky. The moon hovered low and bright. Cold looking, she thought with a shiver. Like ice.

Billy laughed softly from the back of the van. "It doesn't take the moon to make *you* wild, Joey."

"For sure," Dee muttered.

Joey chuckled again. The van picked up speed.

"Sure you're okay, Danielle?" Billy asked.

She turned around in her seat. Billy and Kit were both watching her.

Kit's dark brown hair blended with the shadowy dimness in the back of the van. But his eyes—a pale blue, surrounded by thick black lashes—narrowed with concern.

Billy was worried, too. Danielle could see it in his hazel eyes and the frown on his high forehead. He's such a great guy, she thought. Great looking, too. Dark-blond hair, an athletic body, a dimple when he smiled.

"I'm all right, I guess," Danielle told him. "I—I'm sorry. I know you guys were asleep. I didn't mean to freak everybody out like that."

"Hey, no problem," Billy assured her. "Your scream was better than an alarm clock. And this is a rock band, right? We're supposed to be a little freaked-out."

"Maybe that's what we should call ourselves," Caroline said. "A Little Freaked-Out."

Mary Beth shook her head. "I don't like it."

Caroline laughed. "I was kidding, Mary Beth."

"Hey, how about the Un-nameables?" Joey called out. "You like that one, Danielle?"

"Drive, Joey," Billy ordered. "Just drive." He leaned forward. "Don't pay any attention to Joey," he whispered loudly to Danielle. "We hired him for his muscles, not his brain."

"I heard that!" Joey pretended to be insulted.

Danielle forced a smile. She knew they were trying to cheer her up.

It was working.

But not completely.

If only she could stop having these horrifying, lifelike fantasies.

Danielle leaned her head back and closed her eyes.

"Feeling better?" Caroline whispered.

"A little," Danielle replied. "I just wish I understood what's happening to me. Why do I keep having these awful hallucinations?"

"You can blame Joey for this one," Caroline told her, tucking a strand of long blond hair behind her ear. "He was driving too fast. Everybody knows how nervous you get on the road. I mean . . . ever since your parents' accident."

Danielle felt a lump in her throat. It happened every time she thought about her mother and father.

Almost three years ago Mr. and Mrs. Verona were driving home from a convention when their car spun out of control. It broke through a metal guardrail—and tumbled over a cliff onto rocks fifty feet below.

It happened on a night like this, Danielle thought. On a road like this. Clear and dry. Moonlit.

But it wasn't a fantasy.

Her parents had died.

They had both been thrown from the car. The rocks had slashed them like blades.

No! Danielle told herself. Aunt Margaret never said they were cut up. She never told me any details. I'm just imagining that part.

Imagining the worst.

"I still can't believe it happened," Danielle whispered to Caroline. "It was night, and Dad was used to driving at night. And he was such a careful driver. I mean, he never went even a mile over the speed limit. I used to tease him about getting a ticket for being *too* cautious!"

Caroline shook her head sympathetically. "The fantasies started after the accident, didn't they?"

Danielle nodded. The fantasies were like nightmares. But she wasn't asleep when they happened. She was wide awake—and terrified.

"Have you talked to Dr. Moore about them?" Caroline asked.

Danielle sighed. "What *haven't* I talked to him about?"

She had been seeing Dr. Moore since the accident. The psychiatrist was trying to help her get to the bottom of the fantasies. "Once we find out what's causing them, Danielle," he told her, "they will stop."

I hope he's right, Danielle thought. And I hope it happens soon.

The fantasies were getting worse. More real. More violent.

"I'm sure he'll be able to help," Caroline told her. "Just stick with him."

"Don't worry," Danielle said. "I'm not going to quit him. He asks too many questions, but I guess he has to. And he's smart. He was the one who said the band would be good for me. He was right. If I didn't have the band, I'd really go off the deep end!"

Caroline laughed. "The Deep End. How's that for a name?"

"Hey—that's not bad," Danielle replied.

A few minutes later Joey pulled the van into the hotel parking lot. "Last stop!" he announced. "The luxurious Midland Hotel. And across the street—the Rocket Club. Appearing nightly—the No-Name Band. Step lively, folks!"

Yawning and stretching, the group climbed out of the van.

Danielle followed Caroline down. The moonlight painted the street in a shimmering glow.

Her smile faded. She pulled her duffel bag against her chest and shivered.

Something is wrong, Danielle thought.

My body—it feels so weird.

The cold. I can feel the cold sweeping down over me.

Something strange is happening to me. Something . . . terrible.

She turned to see Caroline staring at her, her blue eyes wide with shock.

Caroline sees it too! Danielle realized.

"Caroline!" Danielle cried, shivering violently. "What is happening to me? What *is* it?"

Chapter 3

I'M WARNING YOU!

"What is it?" Danielle demanded. "Tell me!"

Caroline raised her eyes. "It's your hair, Danny. It's standing straight up!"

"Huh? Standing up?" Danielle dropped her duffel bag and lifted her hands to her head.

She wore her brown hair in a blunt, chin-length cut. Fine and straight, it usually hung like a smooth helmet.

But not now.

Now every strand stuck straight up, as if a powerful fan were blowing from beneath her.

It felt different, too. Not fine and silky, but thick. Rough and bristly.

"It—it must be the wind," Caroline stammered,

still staring. Her own hair, long and blond, lay motionless on her shoulders.

"There isn't any wind!" Danielle cried. Frantically she tugged at her hair, trying to make it lie flat again. "It won't come down! This is *so weird!*"

"Please, Danielle, calm down," Caroline insisted. "It's kind of funny. I mean. It isn't a tragedy—you know. Come on, let's go inside."

Funny? Danielle thought. No. It's not too funny. I feel too strange for it to be funny.

Danielle groaned. A low, guttural noise that didn't even sound like her own voice.

"Come on, let's go into the hotel," Caroline urged. She handed Danielle her duffel bag and guitar. "It's been a long drive. You'll feel better inside."

The Midland Hotel wasn't exactly luxurious. A small lobby contained three chairs arranged around a low chipped table. Plastic plants. A worn rug.

But it was clean. And warm, Danielle thought gratefully as she followed Caroline inside. A ceiling fan spun lazily overhead. The warm draft stirred her hair and blew a strand across her cheek.

She tucked the strand behind her ear and realized that her hair had fallen back to normal.

The strange feeling of cold seemed to seep out of her skin. She wasn't shivering anymore.

She took a deep breath and felt her muscles relax.

"It feels like a sauna in here!" Dee complained, setting her bag down with a thump. "I sure hope the rooms are air-conditioned or I'll never get any sleep."

A drowsy, bald-headed clerk eyed her from behind the check-in desk. "You want air-conditioning, go to the Hilton," he informed her dryly. "You want cheap, you're in the right place."

Dee frowned, but Caroline laughed. "We're definitely in the right place," she told the clerk. "Until we're famous, that is."

"You must be the band." The clerk frowned. "Going to be famous, huh?"

"Yes, we are," Mary Beth assured him seriously. "Just keep reading the newspapers."

"How can he?" Dee muttered. "We don't have a name for him to watch for."

"Okay, everybody, listen up!" Billy strode into the lobby, rubbing his hands together energetically. "Kit and Joey went over to the club. Why don't you unpack, then come on over and check the place out?"

"Good idea," Dee said. "Maybe the club has air-conditioning."

Caroline exchanged a glance with Danielle. "That's Dee. Gripe, gripe, gripe," she whispered.

Danielle grinned. At least she wasn't sharing a room with Dee, she thought. *The way Dee feels about me, she'd probably be at my throat before the night's over.*

The room resembled the lobby. Small, faded, and cheap. But clean and warm.

"Hey, the mattress isn't lumpy!" Caroline announced, flinging herself onto one of the twin beds. "Remember the last place we stayed at?"

Danielle groaned as she set her guitar down. "I felt as if I were lying on a bunch of golf balls."

"Maybe our luck's changing." Caroline scooted off the bed and tossed her bag onto it. "Let's hurry and go check out the Rocket Club."

The two girls quickly unpacked their bags, then took the slow-motion elevator down to the lobby.

Mary Beth and Dee waited for them impatiently. Caroline and Mary Beth hurried toward the door. But Dee hung back a second, grabbing Danielle by the arm.

"I have to talk to you," Dee whispered urgently.

Danielle flinched as Dee's nails dug into her bare skin. "Hey, you're hurting me! Let go!"

But Dee's fingers tightened even harder. "You'll be sorry," she whispered, bringing her face close to Danielle's. "You'll be sorry."

Chapter 4

FIRST KISS

"**W**hat do you mean?" Danielle demanded.

Dee's golden brown eyes narrowed to slits. She opened her mouth to reply. But Caroline's voice interrupted.

"Get a move on, guys!" Caroline called over her shoulder. "You coming?"

"Danielle—" Dee started.

"Give me a break, Dee," Danielle snapped. "I don't know what your problem is. But I'm really sick of your attitude."

She wrenched her arm loose and strode across the lobby. Unfortunately, she *did* know what Dee's problem was.

Dee hated her.

"What was *that* about?" Caroline asked as she pushed open the door.

"Dee's ego," Danielle replied.

"She's still can't handle your being in the group?"

Danielle nodded. "But I've decided to ignore her little outbursts from now on. Let's forget it, okay?"

As they crossed the street, Danielle began to shiver again. She picked up her pace, anxious to get inside.

Billy was waiting for them inside the Rocket Club. "This place is fantastic!" he shouted over the blare of music from the jukebox. "And it holds over a hundred people. Biggest club we've ever played!"

Dee grabbed his hand. "Come on! Let's dance!" She pulled Billy into the middle of the crowded dance floor. Caroline and Mary Beth headed to the bar to get Cokes.

Danielle hung back, gazing around. The Rocket was jammed with laughing, sweating, dancing bodies. Ribbons of green and purple neon light snaked across the ceiling and up and down the walls. Music thundered in her ears.

Danielle skirted the crowd and found an empty table about the size of a quarter. She sat on a wobbly chair and gazed at the low stage.

Couples were dancing to CDs tonight. But tomorrow we'll be up there, she thought. She smiled eagerly.

"Wow, I like that smile," a voice purred in her ear.

Danielle jumped.

Joey leaned over her. His long, curly black hair brushed her cheek.

"Joey!" She edged away. "Sneak up on me, why don't you?"

He chuckled and sat astride the other chair. "How come you never smile like that for me?" he asked.

Danielle wasn't in the mood to flirt. Not with Joey, anyway. "You drive too fast," she told him. "You deliberately try to scare me. I know you do."

Joey stuck his dark glasses on top of his head and peered at her with gray eyes. "How about if I slow down?" he offered.

Danielle shook her head.

"Oh, give me a break." Joey shifted his chair closer. "Let's dance, okay? I'm not a bad guy. Really."

"Thanks, but I don't think so, Joey. I'm kind of tired from the drive."

"You didn't look tired a minute ago," Joey commented. His arm snaked around the back of her chair. His fingertips brushed her bare shoulder.

"I was thinking about tomorrow," Danielle explained. "You know. Playing in front of a crowd like this."

Joey kept rubbing her shoulder. "How about playing for an audience of one?" he suggested softly. "We could go to my room. You could sing for me."

Annoyed, Danielle shrugged his hand off her shoulder. "Give it up, Joey. Okay?" She faked a yawn. "I think I'll go back to the hotel and go to sleep."

Danielle scooted her chair back and stood up.

Joey grabbed her arm. "You know what I think?" he asked. "I think you're scared." He grinned and wiggled his eyebrows. "Nothing to be scared of, Danny. I don't bite. Come on. Take a chance."

"I'm not scared, Joey," Danielle replied sharply. "But I'm starting to get really angry."

Billy suddenly appeared across the table. "Something wrong?" he demanded.

Joey quickly let go of Danielle's arm. "Nothing's wrong," he told Billy. "Everything's cool."

"Good." Billy jerked his thumb over his shoulder. "Kit needs some help backstage," he informed Joey. "Something about the wiring."

Joey nodded unhappily. "Right." He pointed a finger at Danielle. "Save a dance for me, okay? When you're not so *tired.*"

"Right." Danielle let out a sigh of relief as Joey left.

"He comes on kind of strong, doesn't he?" Billy remarked, taking Joey's chair.

"*Strong* isn't the word," Danielle replied, shaking her head. "He comes on like an animal."

"Yeah. I guess," Billy agreed. "I'll talk to him about it."

"No, don't," Danielle told him. "I can handle Joey."

But could she handle Dee? Danielle wondered.

Billy frowned. "If he bothers you again, let me know. Joey knows not to mess with me."

"No one would ever mess with you, Billy," Danielle teased.

"Enough about Joey," Billy replied, tapping the tabletop. "What do you think of the club?"

"It's great!" Danielle exclaimed. "Before Joey came over, I was imagining standing on the stage in front of a crowd like this."

"Nervous?" Billy asked. His dimple flashed in his cheek.

"Always," she confessed. "I try not to be, but I can't help it."

"It doesn't show," he assured her, leaning close to make himself heard over the music. "You've got great energy on the stage. And you're a terrific singer. The band's lucky to have you."

"Thanks, but I'm the lucky one," Danielle said. "I never thought I'd get a chance like this." She gazed around the crowded room, smiling.

Then she saw Dee.

Even from across the room, Danielle could see the angry glitter in Dee's eyes.

Dee's glance shifted to Billy, then back to Danielle.

Oh, great, Danielle thought. Does Dee have something going with Billy?

"Hey, guys," a voice interrupted Danielle's thoughts. She glanced up and into the pale blue eyes of Kit Kragen, the band's equipment manager.

Kit was definitely one of the best-looking guys around, Danielle thought, smiling at him. Tall, with high cheekbones and a strong jaw. Dark, dark hair. And those ice-blue eyes, ringed with long black lashes.

"Hey, Kit," Billy said. "Got the amps up?"

Kit nodded. "I was worried about power for the bass amp. That sucker takes a lot of juice. But it checked out okay. Now I can relax."

"Going back to the hotel?" Billy asked.

"I could use a walk and some air first." Kit turned to Danielle. "I noticed a little park when we were driving in. It's about two blocks away. Feel like taking a walk with me?"

Danielle was surprised. Kit hadn't paid much attention to her so far. He was nice, but kind of distant.

"How about it?" Kit asked.

Danielle felt herself nodding. She couldn't have said no if she'd wanted to. "A walk sounds great," she answered. "Especially after riding in the van for so long."

Kit smiled as Danielle stood up.

No wonder all the fans scream when they see him, she thought. Whatever Kit's magic is, it's working on *me* too!

She glanced at Billy and caught a surprised look on his face.

He must think I'm acting like a groupie, she thought, secretly pleased.

"See you back at the hotel," Kit told Billy. He took Danielle's hand and guided her through the maze of dancers.

As they neared the door, Danielle spotted Dee. Dee had her eyes on Kit, an intense expression on her face.

It's not Billy she wants, Danielle suddenly realized. It's Kit. Dee's jealous of my singing. Now she's going to be jealous about Kit.

Dee's gaze followed Kit all the way to the door. But he didn't seem to notice.

Outside, Kit kept hold of Danielle's hand. His grip was firm and warm.

But Danielle shivered.

"Cold?" Kit asked, turning to her.

"A little." Danielle glanced up. No more clouds to block the moon.

Kit released her hand and slipped his arm around her shoulder. "Should we get you a sweater or something?"

It's not the wind, Danielle thought. There isn't any wind.

It's me.

When they reached the park, Kit led her to a stone bench. It was surrounded by trees. Silvery moonlight filtered through the leaves.

"It's pretty here," Danielle commented, trying to sound enthusiastic.

"Quiet too." Kit snickered. "Maybe I'm in the wrong business. The noise really gets to me sometimes."

Danielle forced a smile. What is going on? she asked herself. Here I am, alone with Kit. I should be really excited.

Instead, she felt cold. Cold and strange.

She raised a hand to her hair. She could feel it bristling again.

But Kit wasn't looking at her hair.

His blue eyes were fastened on Danielle's. They glowed with intensity. "I've been wanting to be alone with you for a long time, Danielle," he whispered. He smiled and leaned forward.

32

All Danielle could see was the light in his eyes.

Kit leaned even closer and kissed her. Danielle kissed him back.

You've stopped shivering, she thought to herself. You're warm again.

She felt the blood rushing through her veins and kissed him harder.

Harder.

He seemed a little surprised but pressed his lips against hers.

Danielle shut her eyes and kissed harder.

Kit screamed as Danielle bit down hard on his lip.

Chapter 5

FIRST BLOOD

Gasping, Kit leaped up from the bench. He uttered a groan and gently pressed a hand against his lips.

What have I *done?* Danielle wondered, suddenly trembling all over. Why did I *do* that?

She gazed up in horror. Blood trickled from Kit's lips, between his fingers.

The blood shone black in the moonlight.

"Danielle?" Kit whispered hoarsely. His expression revealed his confusion. "Why—?"

"I'm sorry!" Danielle choked out. She jumped to her feet, her heart pounding. "I don't know what happened! I'm sorry!"

Kit held out his hand, but Danielle pushed past it. Then, almost without realizing it, she started to run,

run through the cold silver moonlight toward the hotel.

She swallowed hard. Once. Twice. She could taste Kit's blood in her mouth.

Why did I do that? she asked herself again. Why did I bite him so hard?

Why? Why?

A frightening thought made her shudder: *I enjoyed it.*

I enjoyed biting his lip as hard as I could.

The hotel clerk glanced up as Danielle raced breathlessly into the lobby. She turned her face away and hurried to the elevator.

She punched the button, then wiped her mouth with the back of her hand. A smear of Kit's blood came off on her hand. She shuddered again.

By the time she burst into her room, hot tears ran down her cheeks.

"Danielle!" Caroline cried, turning from the closet. "What happened?"

I can't tell her, Danielle thought. How can I tell her I tasted Kit's blood and *enjoyed* it?

Caroline belted her blue terry-cloth robe around her slim figure and crossed the room to Danielle. "What happened?" she repeated, placing a hand on Danielle's arm. "You're so cold, Danny. And are you—are you crying?"

Danielle swallowed. "I have to see Dr. Moore," she managed to say. "Caroline, something's wrong with me."

Concern filled Caroline's blue eyes. "Did you have another fantasy?"

"Sort of." Danielle couldn't make herself tell the real story.

"Violent?"

"Yes!" Danielle cried. "Worse than ever. Caroline, I have to see Dr. Moore tomorrow. He's the only one who can help me!"

"Then you'll see him," Caroline assured her. "We'll talk to Billy about getting you a ride. Don't worry, Billy will be cool about it."

"But our rehearsals," Danielle protested.

"We don't go on until eight at night," Caroline reminded her. "There'll be plenty of time for you to drive to Shadyside and back."

Danielle hoped Caroline was right about Billy letting her go. She *had* to see Dr. Moore.

"You're shaking," Caroline commented. "Listen, I as about to take a shower, but you take one first. It'll warm you up."

In the tiny shower stall Danielle turned the water up as hot as she could bear it. The almost-scalding spray warmed her skin, but the memory of her kiss in the park still chilled her.

Would something else happen before Dr. Moore could help her?

Something worse?

Out of the shower she wrapped up in her long yellow robe. In the mirror her dark eyes were enormous, her face pale. Her hands were still shaking as she pulled a comb through her hair.

After Caroline disappeared into the steamy bathroom, Danielle began to pace the bedroom. She couldn't calm down. She couldn't stop her heart from pounding.

Then she spotted her guitar case.

Maybe music will help, she thought.

She pulled the guitar out and sat on the end of her bed. Out the window she could see the moon. A circle of ice in the sky.

Her fingers strummed the strings. The guitar wasn't hooked up to an amplifier, so the sound was muted. But it didn't matter. She could hear the notes clearly in her head, and that was all she needed.

She kept strumming. No tune at first. Just a few soft chords.

But as she gazed at the moon, she heard a melody in her mind. A melody—and lyrics. With no hesitation, no searching for the right note, she played and sang her new composition.

> "Bad moonlight, falling over me,
>   Bad moonlight, shining down on me,
>   Bad moonlight
>   Makes me feel so strange and new.
>
> "Bad moonlight, falling over me,
>   Bad moonlight, shining down on me,
>   Bad moonlight—
>   I want to die for you!"

How totally weird, Danielle thought as she finished. I've never written anything so easily. It was like magic.

"Danielle, that song—it's awesome!" Caroline exclaimed from the bathroom doorway. "When did you write it?"

"Just now," Danielle told her. "It sort of came to me. All at once. I didn't even have to work on it. Do you really like it?"

"Like it? I love it! It's absolutely the best song you've ever written!" Caroline grinned. "Bad moonlight—sounds really wicked!"

Wicked, Danielle thought. Exactly. In a flash she realized that it was the moon that had been making her feel so strange. So cold.

But why? What was so bad about the moonlight?

"I'm going to call the others in here so they can hear it." Caroline pulled the damp towel from her head and grabbed the telephone.

A few minutes later the rest of the group crowded into the room. Dee wore her robe, but the rest of them were dressed. Joey's clothes were rumpled, as if he'd fallen asleep in them.

"This better be good," Joey said with a yawn. "I was having a great dream when you called. In the dream these two girls—"

"Joey, no one cares," Billy cut him off.

"Wait till you hear it," Caroline declared. "Go ahead, Danielle. Play it."

Danielle strummed an opening chord, then launched into the song. When she finished, no one moved or said anything.

Then Billy started clapping his hands and everyone

joined in. Joey whistled and stomped his feet. Mary Beth's green eyes glowed with excitement. Only Dee refused to join in the applause.

Kit squeezed Danielle's shoulder. "It's a killer," he told her. "A killer!"

"Thanks, Kit," Danielle murmured uncomfortably. She glanced up and saw the dark bruise on his lip. Feeling embarrassed and guilty, she turned away.

Dee was staring at Kit. "How'd you cut your mouth?" she asked him. "Have you been opening beer bottles with your teeth again?"

"My razor slipped," he replied casually, not glancing at Danielle.

Dee squinted at him. "You shave at night?"

"Didn't get a chance this morning," Kit replied. He rubbed his lip tenderly.

Dee shook her head suspiciously.

Oh, wow, Danielle thought unhappily. Dee is crazy about Kit. Now she has another reason to hate me.

"Just call me a klutz," Kit said, sighing.

"Well, just call *us* Bad Moonlight!" Caroline exclaimed. "It's the perfect name for our band—Bad Moonlight! What do you think?"

"Sounds kind of evil." Mary Beth raised an eyebrow and smiled. "I love it."

"What about you, Dee?" Caroline asked.

Dee shrugged. "Like anyone cares what I think," she replied with a scowl.

"Hey, this is excellent! We have a name!" Billy exclaimed. "Now I can tell the club manager how to introduce you. And speaking of the club," he added, "we've got rehearsal at eight-thirty. That's A.M., not P.M. Everybody better get some sleep."

The group made their way out, and Caroline followed them. "I'll talk to Billy about getting you a ride to Shadyside tomorrow," she called to Danielle.

Alone in the room Danielle put her guitar away. She still felt edgy. Tense.

She climbed into bed and closed her eyes. Immediately she saw Kit, standing in front her, his lip bleeding, the blood black in the moonlight.

Think about something else, Danielle scolded herself. Anything else. She turned onto her side, bunching the pillow under her head.

She thought about her new song. "Bad Moonlight." Strange. She'd never written anything like it. Was it really a killer song as Billy had said? Did they all really think it was as good as they said?

Thinking about how easy it was to write the song, she drifted to sleep.

An animal wail shattered the silence.

Danielle's eyes snapped open.

Did she dream it?

She waited. Alert. Listening.

"Ohhh." Danielle realized it hadn't been a dream.

She held her breath as another frightening howl rose up outside her window.

"What's out there?" she cried aloud. "What's making that hideous sound?"

Chapter 6

SCRATCH SCRATCH

Silence.

Then another high-pitched howl.

"Caroline?" Danielle whispered. "Do you hear that?"

No answer from the other bed. Danielle fumbled for her clock on the bedside table.

Midnight.

She'd been asleep for only twenty minutes. Is Caroline still talking to Billy about my ride? Danielle wondered.

Another howl, mournful this time. The howl of a wild animal. So close. So very close.

Joey flashed into her mind. Joey was always tossing back his head and howling like a wild wolf.

Danielle crossed the room in the dark. Reluctantly she pulled up the blind and peered out the window.

Cold, bright moonlight poured over the buildings and the street.

Danielle's scalp prickled. To her surprise, she felt a sudden urge to run outside. To join in the howling.

No! she scolded herself.

What are you *thinking* of?

She pulled the shade down, covering the window.

Back in bed she curled up and tried to ignore the howls.

Another sound made her sit up.

A soft, urgent rap on the door.

"Danielle!"

Dee's voice, calling in a hoarse whisper. "Danielle—I have to talk to you. Now!"

Danielle held her breath and settled back down. No way, she thought angrily. No way I'm letting Dee in.

Why should I talk to Dee? Danielle asked herself.

So Dee can tell me how much she hates me for joining the band and being the lead singer? Danielle already knew Dee was her enemy. She didn't have to hear Dee spell it out.

"Danielle!" Dee whispered again. "I know you're in there." Her knuckles rapped on the door. "Open up, Danielle. Now!"

Go away, Danielle silently begged. Just go away.

After a few more raps, Dee gave up.

Silence in the hall.

Outside, another frightening howl cut through the still summer air.

Danielle tightened her grip on the steering wheel of the borrowed car and peered anxiously at the road sign up ahead. Forty more miles to Shadyside. In less than an hour she'd have a talk with Dr. Moore.

Caroline was right—Billy had been cool about letting her take off after rehearsal. He knew one of the waiters at the club and talked him into letting Danielle borrow his car.

Danielle shook her head. Billy was probably glad to get rid of her. She'd been rotten at rehearsal. Her timing stank and her voice sounded puny. Her fingers felt as clumsy as sausages on the guitar strings.

"Hey, don't think about it," Billy told her during a break. "A bad run-through means a good show."

"Well, in this case it means a *great* show!" Danielle joked. "This run-through is really the pits."

Of course Dee had given Danielle a hard time. "What's your problem?" Dee demanded. "Wild night?"

"No, I crashed early," Danielle told her. She didn't want Dee to know she'd heard her knocking. And she decided not to mention the howls. No one else in the group had mentioned hearing them. They all looked wide awake and rested. "It's just nerves. I'll be fine tonight."

Dee glared at her, but kept quiet.

"You'll be better than fine," Kit told Danielle as he

untangled the cord on the guitar amp. "Your new song's going to kill everyone!"

Danielle felt her face flush. How could Kit be so friendly after what she'd done to him? She wished she could go back in time and erase it.

She felt a powerful attraction to Kit. But even though he still smiled at her a lot, he probably never wanted to be alone with her again.

Sighing, Danielle steered the car around a curve on the road. Forget about Kit for now, she told herself. Get to Dr. Moore. Get help.

Half an hour later Danielle joined the stream of cars on Division Street in Shadyside. She passed rows of stores and three-story office buildings, then turned onto Park Drive and drove into North Hills.

She wished she could visit her brother and her aunt. But there wasn't time. Once she saw Dr. Moore, she had to drive straight back to Midland.

Dr. Moore's office was in his house, a huge gray Victorian near the river. Danielle pulled the car to a stop under the side portico and ran up the steps to the door.

A bell announced her entrance. The receptionist wasn't at her desk. Danielle flopped down in one of the soft beige chairs and picked up a magazine.

Almost immediately she tossed the magazine aside and jumped up. She was too nervous to sit.

Something's happening to me, she thought. Something bad. I have to find out what. And why.

"Danielle?" A smooth, deep voice broke into her thoughts.

"Dr. Moore!" Danielle stopped pacing and spun around.

The doctor stood in the door of his office. A tall bear of a man with a fringe of graying hair around his head. Bright blue eyes beneath bushy gray brows.

His clothes were always slightly rumpled. His glasses were always smudged.

"I tried to call, but the line was busy," Danielle explained. "I know you've got other patients, but you have to squeeze me in." She tried not to sound desperate. But her voice came out shrill and breathless.

Dr. Moore waved her toward his office. "Another patient canceled. Come in, Danielle."

The tall French windows of the large room faced the backyard. A small swimming pool filled the center of the yard. A line of trees separated the pool from the river.

Bookcases lined two of the office walls. Colorful posters of flowers hung on the others. Two deep, soft armchairs faced the desk.

Dr. Moore motioned Danielle into one of the chairs, then sat on the edge of his desk.

"What happened?" he asked.

Barely pausing for breath, Danielle told him about the violent fantasy she experienced in the van. The strange song she wrote about the moonlight. And the frightening scene in the park with Kit.

"*That* wasn't a fantasy!" she cried. "I actually bit him. I drew blood!"

"Are you attracted to Kit?" Dr. Moore asked.

45

"Yes, but—"

The doctor held up his hand. "And is he attracted to you?"

"I think so. At least, he *was,*" Danielle replied.

Dr. Moore smiled. "Two young people, kissing in the moonlight. Teeth sometimes get in the way, you know. Perhaps Kit turned his head slightly?"

Danielle felt a surge of hope.

"It's highly unlikely that you acted violently," Dr. Moore assured her.

"Maybe you're right," Danielle agreed. "But what about these terrible fantasies I have? They're so violent!"

"Yes, let's think about them," Dr. Moore suggested. "Ready to clear your mind?"

Danielle nodded and closed her eyes.

The doctor started to hypnotize her. He'd done it many times.

"I want you to start counting backward from one hundred," Dr. Moore whispered. "Shut everything out of your mind as you count. You will feel yourself relax with each number."

Obediently Danielle began to count. "One hundred . . . ninety-nine . . . ninety-eight . . ."

"You're feeling much more relaxed now," the doctor said, his voice almost a whisper. "Your breathing is deep and steady."

As Danielle kept counting, she felt herself sink into the soft cushion. Her hands rested lightly on the chair arms.

"Are you comfortable, Danielle?" the doctor asked. "Is your mind clear?"

"Yes," she murmured.

"Good. Now, let the thoughts flow," he directed. "And tell me what is happening."

Danielle took a long, slow breath. "The moon," she groaned. "The moon is full. It's shining down on me."

"How does it feel?"

"Cold. Icy." Danielle started breathing faster. "I'm running across a field. Running free. Running away from everyone."

"Why are you running?" Dr. Moore asked.

"It feels good to run free," Danielle replied. "But—" Her leg muscles tensed. Her heart began to pound. "But now I'm being chased! Someone is chasing me!"

"How does that make you feel?" he asked quietly.

"Angry. Furious!" Danielle panted. "I feel such rage! I turn to fight. Now I'm fighting. Fighting with someone." She ground her teeth together. "I'm fighting hard! I'm in a total rage. There's a lot of . . . blood. I keep fighting and . . ."

Dr. Moore snapped his fingers. Once. Twice.

Danielle opened her eyes. Saw the bookcases on the walls. The sun outside the window. Dr. Moore gazing at her.

"That was so . . . gross!" Danielle gasped. "See what I mean? These fantasies are getting so strange. So awful."

"There's still a lot of anger inside you," the doctor

47

commented. "And who can blame you? Your parents died unexpectedly. You're angry about it. At them. At the world."

Danielle nodded. She struggled to slow her breathing.

"Don't be frightened of your fantasies. It's good to let your feelings out, Danielle," Dr. Moore told her. "The more you do, the less angry you'll feel."

Was he right? Danielle wondered. Were her violent fantasies harmless? Were they actually helpful?

Danielle still felt shaken. But Dr. Moore had moved to the door. Time for her to go.

She gripped the arms of the chair to push herself up.

And glanced down in shock.

The pale brown fabric of the chair arms lay torn and shredded.

Danielle raised her hands and stared at them in horror.

Scraps of the fabric were embedded under her fingernails.

She had clawed the chair to ribbons.

Chapter 7

A MOONLIGHT RUN

"*B*ad Moonlight!"

The dancing, cheering crowd at the Rocket Club roared and demanded an encore.

"Bad Moonlight!" they chanted. "Again! Bad Moonlight!"

Danielle's face streamed with sweat. Her outfit—a short, red T-shirt dress blazing with sequins—felt like a limp rag. A callus split open on one of her fingers.

She felt fabulous. I could sing all night! she thought happily.

"'Bad Moonlight.' Again!" the crowd cried. "'Bad Moonlight!'"

Laughing, Danielle spun around to the rest of the band. Caroline flipped her long blond hair over a shoulder and pumped her fist. Behind the drums, Mary Beth grinned back at her. Even Dee appeared happy and pleased.

Until she met Danielle's eyes. Then Dee's expression turned hateful.

Danielle tried not to let it bother her. We're a hit, she thought excitedly. The crowd loves us. Loves my song. Wants to hear it again.

"Give it to them!" Billy shouted from offstage. Standing beside him, Joey gave her a thumbs-up.

Danielle whirled back to face the crowd. She glanced at Caroline, who played the opening notes on the keyboard. Mary Beth joined in with the drumbeat.

Danielle tossed her head and launched into "Bad Moonlight."

The crowd roared its approval, then sang along.

> "Bad Moonlight, falling over me,
> Bad moonlight, shining down on me,
> Bad moonlight . . ."

As she sang, Danielle noticed a figure in the crowd. He stood out because he didn't clap or sing like everyone else. He kept perfectly still, watching her.

Kit.

He usually worked backstage when the band was onstage. He must have come out front just to watch me, Danielle thought.

Kit's pale blue eyes glittered with admiration. Not just for Danielle's singing. For Danielle herself.

Dr. Moore *was* right about the kiss, she realized. Kit wouldn't stare at her that way if he wasn't still attracted to her.

Knowing Kit was watching gave Danielle even more enthusiasm. She finished the song with an explosion of energy and passion.

"Bad Moonlight, shining down on me,
Bad Moonlight
Makes me want to die for you!"

"Let's party!" Joey shouted. He stuck on his sunglasses. "Let's party big time!"

It was after one in the morning and the club had closed. But no one in the group could settle down. "Bad Moonlight"—the song *and* the band—had been an incredible success.

"Let's party!" Joey shouted again. He grabbed Dee around the waist and danced her across the stage.

"Get your paws off me!" Dee teased, shoving him away.

Joey shrugged and turned to Mary Beth. To Danielle's surprise, Mary Beth started to dance with Joey.

If Mary Beth is excited enough to dance with Joey, Danielle thought, then we're definitely a hit!

"How's it going?" Billy asked as Danielle packed up her guitar.

"Wiped out." Danielle grinned. "Fantastic!"

Billy smiled, the dimple in his cheek deepening.

"You were really *radical*, Danielle. I guess you don't need me to tell you that."

"You can tell me," Danielle replied. "I love hearing it."

"Hey, what are we going to do?" Caroline asked Billy. "Everybody's in the mood to celebrate."

Billy ran a hand through his dark blond hair. "I hate to tell you, but with this club closed for the night, the hotel coffee shop is the only game in town."

Caroline shrugged. "That's okay. We can party *anywhere* tonight! We're all totally pumped!"

As Caroline turned away, Danielle spotted Kit across the stage. As he coiled the cables, the muscles in his arms flexed under his black T-shirt.

Danielle couldn't forget the look in Kit's eyes when he watched her sing. She wanted to feel that spark again.

She headed toward Kit. But she was halfway across the stage when strong hands grabbed her and spun her around.

"Joey!"

"You're all mine now!" he exclaimed. He tightened his grip and pulled her toward him.

Before Danielle could stop him, he kissed her on the mouth.

She shoved him hard and pulled her face away. "Cut it out, Joey!" she demanded.

"Come on, Danny," he said with a leer. "You know you're hot for my bod!"

"No way!" Danielle protested.

Across the stage she saw Kit make a disgusted face.

He picked up the coiled cables and disappeared backstage.

Great, Danielle thought. I hope Kit doesn't think I *do* like Joey.

"Okay, everybody!" Billy called out, waving a small piece of paper over his head. "I've got our check. We're not millionaires yet, but I think we can spring for a few cheeseburgers at the coffee shop."

Laughing and joking, Danielle and the others finished packing up and left the club.

Danielle realized she couldn't stand the thought of sitting around a table talking. She suddenly felt like running.

Running for miles in the cool night air. Running free.

"Hey, I'm still really wired," she told Caroline as they crossed the street to the hotel. "I think I'll take a quick walk. Order me a cheeseburger, rare."

Veering away from the group, Danielle started down the sidewalk at a brisk pace. In a couple of minutes she'd passed the shops and small office buildings.

The sidewalks ended, and Danielle found herself walking along a dirt path next to a field. Nothing grew in the field except tall weeds.

Moonlight shimmered over the field, turning the weeds silver-gray.

Danielle raised her head and stared up at the full moon.

"Go!" Danielle whispered to herself.

She started to run.

Her shoes pounded the ground as she ran under the moonlight.

The weeds whipped at her legs and dress, but she didn't slow down.

She couldn't slow down.

The moonlight, she thought. Something about the moonlight. *Makes me feel so strange and new.*

A shape loomed in front of her. A wall. Big stones with wrought-iron bars sunk into the top. The wall stood at least five feet high.

Stop, Danielle thought. *Stop!*

She couldn't stop.

She ran at the stone wall. She felt the muscles in her legs tighten and bunch like springs.

And then, she leaped. Off the ground. Soaring into the air.

Over the wall. So easily. Like a dog. Or a horse.

She landed on all fours.

How did I do that?

Breathing hard, Danielle lifted her head and gazed around. She recognized this place. The park where she had kissed Kit. She had run around the outskirts of town and back to the park.

Feeling winded, Danielle braced her hands on the ground. Started to push herself to her feet.

The moonlight washed over her hands.

Only . . . they weren't *her* hands!

Her nails! Her nails had grown by inches. And they were thick and crusty, curling under like claws.

Danielle held the ugly, thick claws in front of her face and stared at them in silent horror.

54

Bad Moonlight, shining down on me.

She heard a sound. Back in the field. Rustling. Breathing. Footsteps.

Someone had followed her!

She leaped to her feet, raising her ugly claws.

"Joey!" Danielle cried. "What are you *doing* here?"

Chapter 8

A BODY IN THE PARK

"Anybody see Joey?" Billy asked the next morning. Danielle sat with Dee, Mary Beth, and Caroline in the hotel coffee shop.

Mary Beth yawned and brushed back her carrot-colored hair. "Try his room," she suggested.

"Right." Frowning, Billy hurried away from their table.

"Who's got the ham omelette?" the waitress asked.

"I do. And coffee," Mary Beth added. Dark circles ringed her green eyes. "Lots and lots of coffee."

The waitress thumped the plate down and strode off toward the coffeemakers.

"It's a good thing we don't have a show to do tonight," Mary Beth muttered. "I'd probably nod out during the first song."

"How late were you guys up, anyway?" Danielle asked.

"Too late," Caroline groaned, pushing her blond hair behind her ears. "I'll be glad to get in the van and sleep all the way back to Shadyside."

"Coffee," the waitress announced, hefting the glass pot.

Danielle picked up her cup and saw a fresh cut on her forefinger. Another split callus.

"What happened to *you* last night?" Dee demanded. "You never came back to the coffee shop."

"I know." Danielle remembered starting off on a walk. Nothing else. "I guess I was more tired than I thought. I really conked out."

"Tell me about it," Caroline replied, rolling her eyes. "I was afraid we'd get a complaint from the hotel about your snoring."

"Joey hasn't shown yet?" Billy asked, returning to their table. Kit trailed behind him. "Joey has to bring the van around so we can pack up."

"So you're surprised he's sleeping late?" Caroline said. "Joey is the best sleeper in the band. He even sleeps while he's driving!"

Kit shook his head. "He wasn't in our room when I got up."

Billy turned to Danielle. "He took off a couple of minutes after you did last night. You didn't run into him, did you?"

Danielle shook her head. "No. I didn't see him."

Dee set her glass down, splashing orange juice onto

the table. "Joey said something about you when he left," she told Danielle.

"About me?"

Dee nodded. Danielle noticed that Dee's hand shook as she mopped up the juice.

"You okay, Dee?" Billy asked.

"Yeah." Dee glanced at Danielle, then lowered her eyes. "Just fine."

"About Joey," Kit reminded everyone.

"Maybe he forgot something over at the club," Caroline suggested.

"Good thinking," Billy told her.

"Managers." Mary Beth sighed. "They think musicians are brainless."

"Yeah." Caroline laughed and waved Billy and Kit away from the table. "Go get Joey and let us finish our breakfast."

"Aren't you eating, Danielle?" Mary Beth asked, forking up eggs and ham. "You use up a lot of strength during a performance, you know. You shouldn't let yourself get weak or anything."

"I won't," Danielle assured her. "I'm just not hungry right now."

It *is* weird, Danielle thought. I usually eat like crazy after a performance.

I can't still be tired after all those hours I slept, she told herself. But she felt as if she had run a marathon. Every muscle ached.

She glanced across the table at Dee. Dee's brown-gold eyes darted nervously away.

Maybe she feels guilty about the way she treats me,

Danielle thought. Maybe there's a way for us to be friends after all.

They finished breakfast. Then the four band members met Billy and Kit in the lobby. Their bags were already there.

"Did you find Joey?" Dee asked.

Billy shook his head, annoyed. "He wasn't at the club. He's not in his room. He'd better show soon—or he's out of a job."

Danielle turned toward the elevator, where Caroline and Kit were whispering intently. Danielle felt a stab of jealousy. Was something going on between the two of them?

She hoped not. Kit attracted her like a magnet.

"We might as well pack up and move out," Billy decided. "Maybe we'll find Joey walking along the road somewhere."

"You know we won't!" Dee broke in sharply.

Danielle glanced at her in surprise. What did Dee mean?

Before Billy could respond, Dee grabbed her duffel bag and rushed out the door.

"What's Dee's problem?" Danielle asked. "We all know she can't stand Joey. Why is she so upset about him?"

Billy shrugged. "Beats me." He turned to Kit and Caroline. "Okay, guys, we're out of here!"

Out on the street Kit and Billy secured the instruments and other equipment to the top of the van. The girls loaded the bags inside.

Danielle started to climb aboard, but stopped as a police car sped by, its siren blaring.

A second black-and-white cruiser followed, wheeling around the corner, its siren like a wild animal howl.

A few seconds later a red-and-white ambulance went screaming by.

"They're heading for the park!" Kit shouted, shielding his eyes as he watched them. "Come on. Let's go see what's up."

He locked the van and trotted in the direction of the park. Danielle and the others followed close behind.

Two police cars and an ambulance, Danielle thought with a shudder. They were sure in a hurry. It's got to be something bad.

As they approached the park, Danielle saw that she and her friends weren't the only curious ones. A few dozen people stood around, craning their necks and asking questions. Two grim-faced police officers tried to keep them back, without much luck.

Dee ran ahead and caught up with Kit. Danielle saw them push their way through the crowd.

"Everybody back!" one of the officers shouted. "Keep your distance!"

A scream rang out.

"That sounded like Dee!" Caroline exclaimed. "What did she see?"

Danielle's heart started to pound.

"I'm not going any farther," Mary Beth declared, stopping a few feet from the edge of the crowd. "Look at all these people. This is sick."

Caroline stopped too. Her face had grown pale. She bit her lower lip tensely.

Danielle kept walking.

"Everybody back! We've got a crime scene here!" an angry police officer shouted. "Get back!"

Danielle reached the edge of the crowd. As she did, a gap opened up and she could see why Dee had screamed.

What was that heaped on the ground?

A body? A human body?

Torn to pieces?

Its clothing—its *skin*—had all been ripped and shredded.

Clawed to death.

This person had to be clawed to death by a wild animal, Danielle thought.

And then she saw the corpse's face.

Joey's face.

PART TWO

CRIES

Chapter 9

A SONG FOR DEE

Three Weeks Later

"*I know* I didn't do it!" Danielle insisted. "I couldn't possibly have done anything like that!"

"You don't have to convince me, Danielle," Dr. Moore stated quietly. "Why are you trying to convince yourself? What on earth makes you think you might have killed Joey?"

Danielle sat tensely on the edge of the chair in Dr. Moore's office. A new chair, she'd noticed when she came in. Dr. Moore never said a word about how Danielle had torn up the old one.

But Danielle remembered. She kept her hands in her lap, twisting them nervously.

"Danielle?" the doctor prodded. "Why do you think you had anything to do with Joey's death?"

"Because of what I've been telling you," she explained. "The horrible, violent fantasies. What if they become real?"

"You had a violent fantasy about Joey?"

She shook her head. "No. But Billy told me that Joey left the club right after I did that night. And Dee said she heard Joey say something about wanting to talk to me!"

Dr. Moore tapped a pencil against his desktop. "That hardly puts you and Joey together," he pointed out.

"I know that, but—" Danielle swallowed hard. "The thing is, I don't remember what happened after I left the others!" she burst out. "My mind's a blank. A total blank!"

She grabbed the arms of the chair, then quickly lowered her hands back to her lap.

"Why can't I remember anything?" she asked.

"Probably because there's nothing to remember." Dr. Moore jotted down a note. "You finished performing. You felt 'wired,' as you put it, and you walked and jogged a long way. Once you finally worked off your excitement, you were exhausted, Danielle. It's not unusual for people in such a tired state to forget things."

Could that be the way it happened? Danielle wondered.

"You're not likely to carry out any of these fantasies," the doctor continued. "You haven't gotten over the violent way your parents were suddenly taken from you. So your mind is filled with violent thoughts."

He leaned forward, his blue eyes intense behind his glasses. "But that does not mean you will commit violent acts."

Danielle glanced down at her hands. They seemed to have a life of their own. Twisting, writhing in her lap.

She couldn't keep them still.

"You're very tense," Dr. Moore observed. "Let's clear your mind, shall we? That should help you calm down."

He came around and sat on the edge of his desk. "Start counting, Danielle," he commanded softly. "With each number you'll feel yourself start to relax."

Danielle leaned back in the chair and began counting backward from one hundred.

The wind blew back Danielle's hair as the van made its way toward another dreary hotel. More greasy food. And another roaring crowd.

Danielle couldn't wait. She felt loose and ready to perform. Her session with Dr. Moore had really helped. She glanced up and caught Kit's eyes in the rearview mirror. He winked at her playfully.

She grinned, warmed by his attention.

"I can't believe we're just driving to the next club as if nothing happened," Dee said bitterly. "Joey was killed. Slashed to pieces, in case you've forgotten. Doesn't anybody care?"

Silence.

Danielle pictured Joey's body. Bloody and torn. She shook her head to clear away the image.

"Sure we care, Dee," Billy said finally. His voice cracked. "You know we do. We just—"

"We have to keep living, you know?" Caroline broke in. "I mean, we can't crawl under a rock or something."

"We should cancel this show," Dee declared.

"Dee, we can't," Kit replied gently. "It would mean breaking our contract. And I think it's the last thing Joey would have wanted us to do."

Dee muttered a reply. Danielle couldn't hear her.

She's really unhappy, Danielle thought. She reached behind her seat and pulled her guitar out of the case.

"I wrote a song yesterday," she announced. She strummed a chord.

"Another one?" Caroline asked. "Danny, you're really on a roll!"

"If it's as good as 'Bad Moonlight,' you can do it tomorrow night," Billy promised. He had booked them at a club called the Roadhouse in Hastings.

"It's sort of a second 'Bad Moonlight,'" Danielle told them. "More upbeat, though. And it's for Dee to sing," she added.

Dee turned around in her seat, her eyebrows arched in surprise.

Danielle smiled at her. Maybe this'll make things better between us, she thought.

"Let's hear it," Kit demanded.

With her fingers, Danielle tapped out a beat on the front of the guitar. Then she strummed a chord and began to sing.

"Stop me, whoa,
      Bad moonlight, stop me,
      Keep me, stop me,
      Hold me like a friend.

Caroline swung her head to the beat, her blond hair swaying. Mary Beth tapped on the seat back, using her fingers as drumsticks. Dee listened intently, her amber eyes locked on Danielle's face.

"Stop me, whoa,
      Bad moonlight, keep me
      In your cold, cold glow,
      Don't let me kill again."

A long silence greeted the end of the song.

Danielle felt her face heat up with embarrassment and confusion. Had she really written those words?

Billy cleared his throat. "Wow," he murmured.

He started to say more. But Dee interrupted him. " 'Don't let *me* kill again'?" She glared at Danielle. "That's a song for *me* to sing? What's that supposed to mean?"

Danielle shook her head. "I don't know. I don't understand it. I just started to sing it and—"

"I didn't kill Joey! *You* did!" Dee shrieked.

With a cry of rage Dee leaped out of her seat and jumped on Danielle.

Before Danielle could struggle away, Dee wrapped her strong, slender fingers around Danielle's throat and started to strangle her.

Chapter 10

LIKE AN ANIMAL

"It was you!" Dee wailed. "It was *you!*"

Her fingers squeezed tighter.

Dee is so strong, Danielle thought. I never realized how strong she is.

She grabbed hold of Dee's hands with both of her own and tried to pry the viselike fingers from her throat.

Dee kept shouting. No words now. Just shrieks of rage.

Despite Danielle's struggles, Dee's grip tightened.

A wave of panic swept over Danielle. Can't breathe! she thought. She's going to strangle me!

She yanked one of Dee's fingers hard, bending it back as far as she could.

Dee gasped and jerked the hand off Danielle's throat.

The van lurched and slowed to a stop.

Danielle gripped Dee's other wrist and pulled. She felt air rush into her lungs. Taking a deep breath, she scrambled to her knees and shoved Dee away from her.

Dee lunged at her again.

"Hey!" Billy's alarmed voice rang out sharply. "Dee, back off! Back off!"

Danielle flung up her arms, blocking Dee's charge. "I didn't do it! I didn't do it!" The words burst hoarsely from Danielle's aching throat.

"Hurry up, Kit. Give me a hand here!" Billy demanded.

Strong hands grabbed Dee's shoulders, pulled her away from Danielle.

Danielle glared at Dee. The other girl struggled in Kit's grip. He held her in the narrow aisle of the van.

"A song for me, huh?" Dee cried bitterly.

"The words just popped into my head!" Danielle told her. "I don't know why. It didn't mean anything, Dee. I wasn't accusing you. It was just a song!"

"Everybody cool it!" Kit shouted. He shook Dee by the shoulders. "Now!"

Danielle forced herself to stay still. Billy loosened his grip. He rested his hand on her trembling shoulder.

Kit glanced around the group. "We've got a show

tomorrow night," he reminded them. "I know we're all still uptight about Joey, but we can't afford to blow this. Everybody needs to stay cool."

Dee breathed hard. Her eyes never left Danielle's face.

She really believes I killed Joey, Danielle told herself. She screamed it over and over. But why? Why does she suspect me?

Danielle rubbed her throat, sore from Dee's powerful grip.

With a shudder, Danielle turned away from Dee's blazing stare.

Mary Beth gazed solemnly at Danielle. Her green eyes glowed in the dim interior light of the van.

Glowed with fear.

Is Mary Beth afraid of Dee? Danielle wondered. Or is Mary Beth frightened of me?

A shaft of lightning split the sky. Thunder boomed like a canon.

Everyone jumped.

"We're in for rain," Kit said, letting go of Dee's arm. "Let's get moving."

No one spoke during the rest of the trip.

The storm followed them the whole ninety-mile drive. Lightning bolts snaked down from the sky. Thunder rattled the windows of the van.

When Kit pulled up in front of the hotel, the rain shot down like bullets.

"Billy and I will need some extra hands with the

equipment!" Kit shouted over the drumming of the rain. "We'll unload the top of the van first!"

He opened the sliding door and jumped down to the street. Billy followed, then Dee, Mary Beth, and Caroline.

When Danielle hopped down to the wet pavement, the rain plastered her hair to her head. Flinging it back, she raised her face to the sky.

"Danielle, come on," Caroline called over her shoulder. "You want to drown?"

But Danielle felt a sudden urge to move.

To run through the storm. To feel the wind and water against her skin.

Squinting against the driving rain, she took off down the street.

"Danny!" Caroline shouted after her. "Where are you going? We have to unpack!"

"Let her go," Danielle heard Kit shout at Caroline. "She'll be okay."

Will I? Danielle wondered. Will I ever be okay?

Her legs churning, she threw herself into the driving curtains of rain. Splashing through puddles. Stumbling and scrambling up again.

What am I doing? she asked herself. I can't stop myself. I can't stop!

The sky cleared as she stopped her frantic run.

Gasping for breath, she slowed to a trot, then a walk. Her side ached. Her legs wobbled like rubber.

Her mouth felt dry. I'm thirsty, she realized.

So thirsty.

I must drink.

Danielle lowered herself to the street.

On all fours she bent over a puddle and frantically lapped the rainwater with her tongue.

Chapter 11

KIT DIES

*A*t rehearsal the next morning, they checked out the club. The Roadhouse wasn't quite as big as the Rocket Club. But the two owners knew each other, and word about Bad Moonlight had spread.

"It'll be packed tonight," the club's manager told Billy when the band took a break. "I warned my bouncers. We'll probably have to turn people away."

Billy grinned. "You hear that, guys?" he called out. "Tonight we've got to really kick!"

The manager jerked his thumb at Danielle. "We got you to thank for it, honey," he told her. "Dave from the Rocket said you were dy-no-mite."

Danielle smiled at him as she tightened a new string on her guitar.

75

Caroline rolled her eyes. *"Honey?"* she whispered to Danielle.

"Dy-no-mite!" Danielle whispered back, laughing.

"Could we get back to work?" Dee demanded impatiently from the other side of the stage. "We've been hanging out for twenty minutes."

Billy nodded. "Sure, Dee. You want to work? We'll work."

"Good." Dee picked up her guitar and frowned at Danielle.

She still thinks I wrote that song to accuse her of killing Joey, Danielle thought. The two of us will never become friends. No way. It's hopeless now.

No one had mentioned putting Danielle's new song into the show, not after what happened in the van. No one talked about what happened, either.

But Danielle couldn't forget the feeling of Dee's fingers on her neck. Squeezing tighter and tighter.

Trying to kill her.

And I didn't just fight back, Danielle thought with a shudder. I wanted to kill *her!*

Violent thoughts, because of what had happened to her parents. Dr. Moore said she wouldn't act on those thoughts.

Danielle was terrified that she would.

After the fight with Dee, Danielle remembered, she had run like a crazy person. She drank from a puddle of dirty rainwater. Lapped up the water like a thirsty dog.

What's wrong with me? Danielle wondered. Something is happening to me, and I don't know how to stop it.

"Danielle, you ready?" Billy asked, breaking into her troubled thoughts.

Danielle jumped. "Sure, Billy. Sorry." She picked up her guitar and jogged toward the front of the stage.

"You okay?" Kit murmured as she passed him, his blue eyes full of concern. "You look worried about something."

Danielle shook her head. She couldn't tell him. How could she tell the guy she liked that she might be going crazy?

"I'm all right," she reassured him. "Just a little tired, I guess."

"Okay!" Billy called out, when Danielle took her place. "Start with 'Bad Moonlight.' Make this place jump!"

For a while Danielle lost herself in the music. It cleared her mind and made her feel safe.

Too bad she ever had to stop.

"Wear the red dress again," Caroline advised Danielle later in their hotel room. "You wore it in Midland and we were a hit."

"I think she ought to wear black," Mary Beth argued. "Those tight black pants and that cropped T-shirt with the silver things on it. They look like half-moons—it'll go with our name."

"I hate those pants," Danielle declared. "I have to lie down to get them on. And I'm always afraid they're going to split up the back."

"That'd make it a full moon!" Caroline joked.

Mary Beth laughed and tossed a pair of rolled-up socks at her. Caroline tossed them back, but Danielle grabbed them in mid-air and threw them at Caroline.

They were still heaving the socks at each other when somebody banged on the door. "Hey, it's me. Open up!" Billy called in.

Caroline opened the door. "What's the matter?"

"I can't find Kit," Billy told them, pushing back a tangle of dark blond hair. "He needs to set up for the show. We're on in an hour and a half. Anybody seen him?"

"I saw him around three, after we finished rehearsing," Mary Beth volunteered. "He was leaving the club with Dee."

"With Dee?" Danielle asked, feeling a twinge of jealousy.

Mary Beth nodded. "They were having some kind of argument. I couldn't hear what they were saying, but it was pretty intense."

Danielle frowned, thinking hard. What could Dee and Kit be arguing about?

Billy glanced at his watch. "We've got to find them. Let's spread out and look. Hastings is small. It shouldn't take us long. Mary Beth, you come with me," he ordered. "We'll look north, up by the river, then west. Danielle, you and Caroline take the south side, then go east."

Danielle pulled on her sneakers and followed the others out of the hotel. "Where could they have gone?" she asked, shoving her hands into the pockets

78

of her cut-offs. "Kit wouldn't take off—an hour and a half before a show."

"I know," Caroline agreed. "It's not like him. It's not like him to argue with anyone, either. Kit's always so calm and cool. I only saw him get mad once, when Joey blew out an amplifier."

They turned a corner and hurried down a side street lined with old brick buildings. Weeds poked through the cracks in the sidewalk.

"Dee's been so totally weird since Joey died," Caroline said thoughtfully. "I mean, she's never exactly the life of the party, but she's been so much moodier and angrier."

"Yeah." Danielle reached up and touched her throat. It still felt sore from Dee's angry attack.

Danielle's heart speeded up. She suddenly had a powerful feeling of dread.

What could Dee and Kit be arguing about? What?

"Hey, Danielle, wait up!" Caroline called. "Why are you walking so fast? This isn't a race!"

"I want to find him!" Danielle called back. "Something's wrong. Something's happened!"

She ran to the end of the block. An abandoned building sat on the right, its windows boarded up.

Danielle glanced across the street. An empty lot. Broken glass littered the ground. The wind blew fast-food wrappers and yellowing newspapers against the rusty fence surrounding it.

Danielle glimpsed a flash of color in the waist-high weeds. Leaping off the sidewalk, she ran across the street—and stared in horror into the empty lot.

Behind the fence, Kit lay on his back on the ground. His face pale. His eyes wide with fear. His shirt ripped at the shoulder.

Her arms crossed over her chest, Dee stood over him.

Kit struggled to his feet and faced her. "Dee," he begged hoarsely. "Please—don't!"

Dee didn't seem to hear him. Her eyes narrowed, she advanced a step. She crouched over, her legs bent at the knees. Her hands flexed, the fingers curved like claws.

Dee's lips drew back in a hideous grin. Her breath came faster. Her golden eyes glinted with savage glee.

"No!" Danielle screamed through the wire fence. "Kit! Dee! No!"

Too late.

Roaring like an animal, Dee dived at Kit, raised both hands, and began slashing him to pieces.

Chapter 12

A SURPRISE IN THE CLOSET

"Nooo!" Danielle screamed again, rattling the fence with both hands.

"Danielle—what's wrong?" Caroline cried. She came running up behind her. "What is it?"

"Kit! Kit!" Danielle continued to shake the rusty fence. "Dee, stop!" she shrieked. "Caroline—she's going to kill him!"

Caroline yanked Danielle's arm hard and turned her around. "What are you talking about? Kit and Dee aren't in there, Danielle! It's just two kids. Look!"

Danielle blinked hard and squinted through the fence.

Two dark-haired boys, about nine or ten, stared back at her. "Hey—we were just wrestling," one of them called to Danielle.

"We weren't doing anything wrong!" the other boy called in a trembling, tiny voice.

"Uh . . . sorry," Danielle murmured.

But the boys didn't wait for her apology. They raced to the other side of the lot, ducked under the fence, and ran out of sight.

Two kids, Danielle thought.

Not Kit and Dee.

Two boys.

She uttered a low moan as she realized she'd had another violent fantasy. So powerful. So real.

"What happened?" Caroline demanded, snapping Danielle from her frightening thoughts. "You screamed about Kit and Dee. You saw something, didn't you?"

Danielle nodded.

"What was it?"

"That doesn't matter!" Danielle cried. "What matters is these fantasies aren't stopping!"

"Come on," Caroline urged, putting an arm around Danielle's shoulders. "Let's get back to the hotel. You told me you met with Dr. Moore. What did he say?"

"He says I have violent thoughts because my parents died violently."

"Well, that makes sense, I guess," Caroline said. She guided Danielle gently back toward the hotel.

As they walked, a picture suddenly flashed into Danielle's mind. Not a fantasy. Something much more frightening.

Once again Danielle saw her parents' accident. Their car soaring off the cliff. Their bodies torn on the jagged rocks below.

She hadn't seen her parents' bodies, not even at the funeral. And no one had told her they'd been torn up on the rocks. But that's what she kept picturing.

Why? she wondered, her hands clenched into fists. Why do I keep thinking about it? Why can't I put it behind me?

She sucked in a long breath.

"Are you going to be okay?" Caroline asked, her blue eyes studying Danielle. "Do you want me to ask Billy—"

"No!" Danielle interrupted. "Don't tell Billy I freaked out again. He probably already wishes I'd never joined the band."

"No way," Caroline declared. "He thinks you're great. But, Danielle, Billy really cares about everybody in the band. He'd want to know if something's wrong."

"I still don't want you to tell him," Danielle insisted. "I'll be okay for the show. Please, Caroline. Promise me you won't say anything to him about this."

"Okay, I won't tell," Caroline promised.

A few minutes later they arrived at the hotel. Danielle saw everyone in the small lobby. To her great relief, Kit and Dee were there, too.

"I can't believe you two would just take off like that!" she heard Billy scolding Kit and Dee. He checked his watch. "We've got a performance in less than an hour, in case you forgot!"

"We didn't take off," Dee snapped. "We're here, aren't we?"

"Hey, I'm sorry, man," Kit told Billy. "I ran into some friends and didn't notice the time. I'll go set up the equipment. Right now. No problem."

Kit squeezed Danielle's shoulder as he hurried past her.

"What about you, Dee?" Mary Beth asked. "Where were you?"

Dee shrugged. "I took a walk."

Mary Beth frowned. "Where?"

"Hey—you're not my mother!" Dee snapped.

"Never mind," Billy said impatiently. "We've got a show to put on. Everybody move it!"

Danielle wore her sparkling red dress for the performance. Maybe it's my lucky dress, she thought as the audience stomped and clapped for an encore of "Bad Moonlight."

"Hey, isn't there a curfew in this town?" she called out, teasing the crowd. "If we sing again, anybody under twenty-one will get picked up."

"We don't care!" a girl shouted. The crowd cheered.

Laughing, Danielle turned to the band. "What do you say? Shall we get them in trouble?"

For an answer Mary Beth tossed her short red hair and did a riff on the drums. Caroline and Dee played the opening bar of the song, and Danielle turned back to the audience. "You want it? You got it!" she shouted.

The crowd cheered.

"Bad Moonlight" killed them again.

"A hit in Hastings!" Billy kept chanting when the show was over. "We're a hit in Hastings!"

"You're not thinking of making that a song, I hope," Caroline said dryly. "If you are, I have to warn you—the lyrics really bite."

Billy laughed. "Don't worry, I'll leave the songwriting to Danielle. I'm just so pumped!" he added as he hurried to help Kit break down the equipment.

"So was the audience," Mary Beth commented. "What an awesome night!"

"Hey, why don't we take a walk or something?" Billy suggested, doing a couple of dance steps as he coiled up a cable. "Let's see what kind of trouble we can get into. I'm not ready to settle down yet."

"Count me in," Kit replied, picking up one of the extra floor mikes. "Let's get this stuff stowed in the van and go down to the river."

They all worked quickly, and in another twenty minutes the equipment was packed.

As Danielle hopped out of the van, she glanced up at the sky. A thin layer of clouds had covered it all evening. Now the clouds had drifted away, revealing a pale moon. Nearly full.

"Hey, it feels great to walk. I mean, after being cooped up in that tiny club," Kit said. He slid an arm around Danielle's shoulder. "Wow. Check out the moon."

Danielle leaned into the circle of his arm. "It's . . . beautiful," she said softly.

Beautiful—and bad, she thought.

Danielle shivered. I can't walk under that moonlight, she told herself.

No more bad moonlight.

The words forced their way through her mind.

Her body began to tremble.

I'm afraid of the moonlight, she realized. Afraid of the bad moonlight.

Afraid of what it will make me do.

"Is everybody ready?" Billy asked, slamming the van doors.

Danielle straightened up and stepped away from Kit. "I think I'll skip the walk," she said, trying to sound casual.

"Huh? How come?" Mary Beth asked. "It's a perfect night to hang out by the river."

"Yeah, come on, Danielle," Caroline urged. "What's your problem? I thought you were as pumped as the rest of us."

"I am," Danielle agreed. She struggled to think of a good excuse not to go.

"Then come with us!" Billy insisted.

"We're wasting time standing around talking," Dee said impatiently. "I'm going on ahead. See you at the river."

"We'll catch up in a minute!" Kit called after Dee.

He turned to Danielle. "I really wish you'd come," he told her.

Danielle felt tempted. The light in Kit's eyes was so warm.

But the moonlight was cold.

Cold and evil.

Danielle knew she had to stay out of it.

"Sorry guys," she insisted, keeping her voice light. "I feel a song coming on. If I don't work on it now, I'll lose it."

The others grumbled, but they didn't push her anymore. Danielle knew they wouldn't. They knew how hard it was to write songs. If an inspiration hit, you had to go with it.

Danielle grabbed her guitar from the van and waved goodbye. She hurried up to her room. Without bothering to turn on any lights, she flung herself across one of the lumpy beds.

Her entire body trembled.

Maybe she *should* try to write a song. She could use the melody from "Stop Me," the one she'd written for Dee, and put some new lyric to it.

She had dropped her guitar by the closet door. Danielle pushed herself off the bed and stumbled toward the closet.

She stopped halfway across the dark room when she heard a sound.

A rustling. Then a cough.

I'm not alone, she realized. There's someone else in this room.

Danielle straightened up and started to back away from the closet.

With a loud creak the closet door swung open.

Dee stepped out into the dim light. Her amber eyes glinted with fury. "Don't even try to get away this time," she whispered.

Chapter 13

MAKE IT STOP!

"Dee—what are you doing here?" Danielle choked out. "I saw you leave for the river."

"Yeah, right," Dee muttered. She clicked on the ceiling light. "You've been trying to avoid me, Danielle. But you can't—not now. Not this time. You and I are going to talk."

"No!" Danielle cried. Dee's intense stare terrified her. "Get out!"

"Listen to me!" Dee insisted, taking a step closer. "I know the truth about Joey!"

"Huh? What are you saying?" Danielle rushed past Dee and pulled open the door to the hallway. "I don't want to hear any more about it! Get out! Get out!"

"Not until we talk!" Dee insisted in a low voice. Moving swiftly, she advanced on Danielle.

With a gasp Danielle turned to flee.

Kit stood blocking the doorway.

"Kit!" Danielle grabbed his arm. "What are you—? Never mind! I'm so glad to see you!"

Kit took a step into the room. He turned to Dee. "What's up? You went with the others."

The fire in Dee's eyes faded. "I changed my mind," she muttered. "Uh . . . I was just saying good night to Danielle. See you guys. Later." Avoiding their eyes, Dee stepped past them and out of the room.

"What was that about?" Kit asked Danielle, drawing her into the room. "You look upset."

"I am!" Danielle exclaimed. "Kit, she was so *furious!* I thought she was going to try to strangle me again. She said she knew the truth about Joey!"

"Excuse me?" Kit's voice came out shrill. "What did she mean by that?"

"I didn't give her a chance to tell me." Danielle drew a shaky breath. "But you heard what she accused me of in the van!"

"Hey, calm down," Kit said gently. Taking her hand, he pulled her toward the window. "Dee's been really upset since Joey died, and—"

"I noticed," Danielle interrupted.

Kit nodded. "Yeah, I guess I don't have to tell you," he admitted. "But anyway, I don't think Dee really means what she says."

"She didn't even like Joey," Danielle insisted. "At least, she didn't act as if she did."

"Some people don't show how they feel," Kit

replied. He put his arm around Danielle again and pulled her close. "I'm not one of them," he confided.

Danielle smiled. "I'm glad you're not," she whispered.

Kit bent his head and kissed her.

Danielle kissed him back, enjoying the moment.

A warm breeze blew through the open window, but Danielle shivered. She opened her eyes.

Moonlight streamed in, bathing them both in its icy glow.

Ignore it, she told herself. Enjoy the kiss.

She pressed her hands against the back of Kit's neck.

But pulled away suddenly when she heard the long, mournful howl. So close. Just outside the hotel.

She gasped and stumbled back from the window.

Another terrifying howl.

Danielle covered her ears. "Make it stop!" she cried. "Please, Kit! Make it stop!"

"Huh?" Kit gazed at her with concern. "Danielle—make *what* stop?"

Chapter 14

BILLY DIES

Kit studied her face. "Do you really hear something?"

"I—" Danielle paused. Don't tell him, she thought. Don't let him know. He'll think you're weird. A freak.

"Danielle?"

"No," Danielle said. "I mean, yes. I heard *something*. A truck, I guess. You know, one of those monster trucks, roaring past."

"I didn't hear it." Kit shrugged and reached for her again.

"Listen, Kit, maybe you should go to the river with everybody else," Danielle told him. "I was going to work on a song, but I suddenly feel really wiped."

She could see the disappointment on Kit's face. "You sure you're okay?" he asked.

"Yeah. I'm okay." Danielle put her arm around his waist and urged him to the door. "I'm really glad you came back, Kit."

"Me too." Kit leaned close and kissed her. "See you tomorrow. And try not to worry too much about Dee."

Right, Danielle thought as she closed the door behind him. I won't worry *too* much about Dee. After all, I have a good list of other things to worry about.

Like the horrifying fantasies.

My parents' car accident.

The strange animal howls that no one else seems to hear.

The moonlight. The bad moonlight . . .

Danielle lowered the shade on the window to shut out the moonlight. She slid the red dress off and slipped into the faded blue, oversize T-shirt that she liked to sleep in.

The howling had stopped for the moment. Maybe she'd be able to sleep. Then she could forget everything for a while.

Danielle climbed into bed, pulled the sheet up, and closed her eyes.

The howling began again.

Ignore it. It's in your mind, she scolded herself.

No. It's not. It's real.

She buried her head in the pillow, forcing away the frightening wails.

She fell into a fitful, dreamless sleep. Woke fully alert a little after two.

Caroline?

93

No. Still not back.

Why was Caroline out so late?

Restless and wide awake, Danielle jumped out of bed. I'll get a soda from the machine at the end of the hall, she decided. Then maybe try to work on a song.

She dug some change out of her duffel bag and pulled open the door.

Danielle froze.

Halfway down the hall, sprawled on the worn carpet, lay a body.

Dark blond hair.

Eyes shut tightly. Mouth hanging slackly open.

Not smiling.

Not smiling with the dimple in his cheek.

Not smiling. Not smiling. Not smiling.

No. Billy wasn't smiling.

Billy was dead.

Chapter 15

VERY WORRIED ABOUT
DANIELLE

Not Billy, Danielle thought. *Please,* not Billy!

It's a fantasy, she told herself, trembling all over. Another horrifying fantasy.

Danielle squeezed her eyes shut.

I'll open my eyes, and he'll be okay.

I'll open my eyes, and the body will have vanished.

She took a deep breath and opened her eyes.

Still there.

The blood throbbing at her temples, Danielle took a step toward Billy. Then another, and another.

Billy's yellow T-shirt rose and fell on his chest. He was breathing!

Gasping with relief, Danielle ran to him and knelt down.

A sharp smell floated up to greet her. The smell of alcohol.

Then she noticed the can in his outstretched hand. A beer can.

"Billy?" she whispered. She tugged his arm. "Billy!"

He groaned but didn't move.

Billy didn't drink much, she knew. Just a beer once in a while. He never got drunk.

But how much had he drunk tonight? Enough to pass out in the hotel hallway.

Why? Danielle wondered. What would make a responsible guy like Billy suddenly do something like this?

She shook his arm again. "Billy, wake up!"

Billy groaned again. He turned his head, swallowed, and opened his eyes. "Danielle? What . . . what's up? I feel awful." He choked out in a hoarse voice.

"You fell asleep in the hall," she told him. "Come on, I'll help you back to your room." She took his arm and tugged.

With great effort she got Billy on his feet. He squinted around the hall, his expression dazed. The beer can fell from his hand and rolled over the carpet.

"Why'd you drink so much tonight?" Danielle asked. "Partying?"

Billy shook his head. "A lot on my mind."

"Like what?"

Billy didn't reply. Danielle guided him to his room. He leaned against the door, still dazed. He stared at

Danielle, struggling to focus. Then he reached out and pulled Danielle close to him in a hug.

Danielle closed her eyes, enjoying the feeling of his arms around her and his chin resting on her head. "This isn't like you," she whispered. "Tell me what's wrong, Billy."

"I wish I could."

"Why can't you?" she asked. "It can't be that bad."

Billy's hands tightened. Then he straightened up and pushed away from her. "You're wrong," he told her. "It's much worse than you can imagine."

"So tell me!" Danielle insisted. "Maybe I can help."

"I want to, but—" Billy broke off and shook his head. His hazel eyes darkened. "No. You can't help, Danielle. Just forget it, okay?"

"But—"

"I said forget it!" Billy snapped.

Danielle stared at him, startled by his sudden anger.

He muttered good night and stumbled into his room. Danielle stood in the hallway, staring at the closed door, thinking about Billy's troubled words.

In the distance the howling started again.

With a shiver Danielle turned and hurried back to her room.

Tomorrow, she thought, slamming the door behind her and carefully locking it. Tomorrow I'll be home with Aunt Margaret.

Tomorrow I'll be safe.

* * *

"You're awfully quiet, Danielle," Aunt Margaret commented as she sponged off the counter after lunch the next day.

"Yeah, we're lucky!" Cliff snickered and tossed his rolled-up napkin at Danielle.

"Ha, ha, Cliff." Danielle caught the napkin, jumped up from the table, and stuffed it down the back of her brother's T-shirt.

"You jerk!" he cried. He reached behind himself and struggled to pull the napkin out.

Aunt Margaret pulled it out for him. "Cliff—out!" she ordered, rolling her eyes at Danielle. "Go out in the yard and work off some of that energy while I talk to your sister."

"There's nothing to do out there," Cliff complained.

Aunt Margaret sighed. "Cliff, you built a fort out of cardboard boxes yesterday. Don't tell me you're tired of it already."

"Oh, right—the fort," Cliff remembered. "Okay. I'm outta here." He dashed out the back door, making machine-gun noises as he left.

Danielle stacked their lunch plates and carried them to the dishwasher. It felt good to be back in her own house, especially the kitchen. She loved the big square room with its cream-tiled floor, round oak table, and hanging plants in the window over the sink.

"Now," Aunt Margaret coaxed, pouring herself a cup of coffee. "Tell me what's troubling you."

Danielle poured soap powder into the dishwasher.

"I've just been feeling so strange," she replied. "And I keep having these horrible fantasies—people fighting, tearing each other to bits. Dying!"

She slammed the dishwasher closed and turned it on. "I love being in the band, and I hate to let the others down. But maybe I should quit."

Aunt Margaret raised a heavily penciled eyebrow. "You're not a quitter, Danielle."

"I know!" Danielle cried. "But I keep thinking if I went to college now, instead of next year, then maybe things would change."

Aunt Margaret blew on her coffee and took a sip. A film of bright red lipstick came off on the cup. "Here's what I think," she announced. "You should take it easy for a while. When's your next show?"

"In a couple of days."

"Good. Then you'll have some time to clear your mind," Aunt Margaret declared. "Of course, you'll have to rehearse. But no traveling. So do some shopping, go to the movies, sleep till noon if you want. Then see how you feel."

"I already know how I feel!" Danielle exclaimed. "Scared. No, not scared—terrified! Aunt Margaret, these fantasies keep getting more and more violent. And I keep thinking about Mom and Dad. A lot."

"Didn't Dr. Moore say that was to be expected?" Aunt Margaret asked. "That it would take time to get over what happened?"

"Yeah, but it's taking too much time," Danielle insisted. "I don't just miss them, Aunt Margaret. I could stand that, I guess. But I keep seeing them—picturing the car flying off the cliff. Why? Why can't I get it out of my mind?"

Aunt Margaret frowned sadly and shook her head.

"Tell me again about the accident," Danielle begged. "I want to know exactly what happened. I want to know every single detail. Maybe I need to keep hearing about it until I'm sick of it or something."

Aunt Margaret clicked her tongue. "It isn't good to keep dwelling on these things."

"But—"

"No *buts.*" Aunt Margaret crossed to Danielle and put her arm around her. "I'm no expert, but I simply can't believe that hearing about your parents' accident over and over again is going to help you one bit."

Was she right? Danielle wondered. Maybe. But *not* hearing about the accident wasn't helping, either. She couldn't stop thinking about it, no matter how hard she tried.

"Oh, look at the time!" Aunt Margaret exclaimed. "I've got laundry to fold and errands to run, and it's already two o'clock."

"I'll fold the laundry," Danielle offered.

"Absolutely not! I forbid you to do anything but relax and enjoy yourself." Aunt Margaret squeezed Danielle's shoulder. "It'll be the best thing for you."

"I hope you're right."

"Of course I'm right, young lady!" Aunt Margaret said sternly. "Now. Didn't you and Caroline make plans to go to a movie later?"

Danielle nodded.

"Good. Why don't you go out on the patio and relax until it's time to go." Pushing back her dyed red hair, Aunt Margaret bustled out of the kitchen.

Danielle rinsed out the coffee cup and wiped off the table. She glanced out the window. Clear and sunny. But she didn't feel like sitting on the patio.

She didn't feel like going to the movies, either.

Caroline would understand. She knew what Danielle was going through.

Danielle wiped her hands on the dishtowel and reached for the wall phone next to the refrigerator.

Aunt Margaret's voice came over the line. Danielle started to apologize, but Aunt Margaret must not have realized that Danielle had picked up the extension.

Before Danielle could hang up, she heard her own name.

"It's Danielle," Aunt Margaret declared to someone on the other end of the line. "I'm very worried about her. *Very* worried!"

A pause. Then Danielle heard the second voice.

"Come over right now. We must talk about her," the voice insisted. "I'm worried, too."

Danielle stared at the phone in shock.

The second voice belonged to Dr. Moore.

Chapter 16

A BIG SECRET

"Come to my office right now," Danielle heard Dr. Moore repeat.

"I'll be there in fifteen minutes," Aunt Margaret replied. Danielle heard a click as her aunt hung up the receiver.

Stunned, Danielle hung up too. She stared blindly at the telephone, her thoughts racing.

She had no idea that Aunt Margaret ever talked to Dr. Moore. Had she been talking to him all along, ever since Danielle started seeing him? They sounded as if they'd spoken before.

Aunt Margaret thinks I'm getting worse, Danielle thought.

The sound of heels clicking down the hall made

Danielle jump guiltily away from the phone. When Aunt Margaret entered the kitchen, she found Danielle peering into the refrigerator.

Aunt Margaret clicked her tongue. "I thought I told you to go outside and relax in that sunshine."

"I am. I'm just getting something to drink." Danielle grabbed a Coke and turned around. Her aunt was ready to go, a big purse slung over her shoulder and her lipstick freshened.

She looks really tense, Danielle thought. "Did you fold the laundry already?"

"The laundry can wait," Aunt Margaret declared. "I want to get to that white sale at Brady's. Everything is probably picked over by now, but maybe I'll get lucky."

"Sure," Danielle said. "See you later."

"You relax," Aunt Margaret called back over her shoulder as she hurried out of the room.

When Danielle heard the front door slam, she sank down on the nearest chair. She shut her eyes, tried to stop the room from spinning.

Aunt Margaret had lied to her!

After her parents' accident, her aunt had moved all the way across the country to take care of Danielle and Cliff. Aunt Margaret had always been there whenever they needed her.

Danielle trusted her.

Until now.

Aunt Margaret hid the fact that she talked with Dr. Moore about Danielle.

Was she hiding other things?

Danielle rose from the table and gazed out the kitchen window. Cliff and his friend from down the street were playing in the cardboard fort. They'd be at it for hours.

Danielle had the house to herself.

Time to find out if Aunt Margaret had any other secrets.

Danielle stuck the Coke back in the refrigerator and crept out of the kitchen and up the stairs.

Her aunt's room overlooked the front yard. The door was closed.

You shouldn't do this, Danielle scolded herself. Aunt Margaret deserves her privacy.

But I deserve to know if I can trust her.

She turned the knob and pushed the door open.

The small room used to be the guest room. Her aunt refused to take over Danielle's parents' bedroom. That was one of the things Danielle loved about her.

Danielle crossed the room and started with the desk.

The shallow top drawer held pens and pencils, scissors, rubber bands.

The second drawer contained checks and stubs of paid bills, a box of stationery.

Danielle moved down to the third drawer. Deep, with folders jammed in tightly. She pulled one out. Yellowed recipes clipped from magazines and newspapers.

Another folder held blank typing paper. A third was

filled with *Consumer Reports* articles about computers. Cliff wanted one for his birthday, Danielle remembered. Aunt Margaret obviously wanted to find the best one.

Danielle searched through folder after folder, but found nothing interesting or surprising. No secrets.

Good, she thought. Now put this stuff back and get out of here before you get caught.

As she gathered a stack of folders, something on the bottom of the drawer caught her attention.

An envelope, way at the back. Danielle dropped the folders and carefully pulled it out.

The envelope contained a wrinkled newspaper clipping. Dated two days after Danielle's parents had been found dead.

The headline leaped out at her: CAUSE UNKNOWN IN MYSTERIOUS DEATH OF SHADYSIDE COUPLE.

A mysterious death? Danielle's hands started shaking so badly she was afraid she'd rip the paper. Her parents' death wasn't a mystery! They died in a car accident!

Or did they?

Was this another secret? Another lie from Aunt Margaret?

Danielle crossed the room and sat down in the rocking chair. She didn't want to read the story, but she had to. She had to find out what really happened to her parents.

Smoothing the paper out on her knees, she began to read:

The bodies of Shadyside residents Michael and Abigail Verona were discovered early Wednesday morning in a rock-strewn ravine twenty miles from town. The couple had been returning to Shadyside in their car.

It is thought that a flat tire caused them to stop. What happened after that remains a mystery to local police.

All that is certain is that they were clawed to death, their bodies torn apart.

When questioned by reporters, a highway patrolman on the scene stated grimly, "It looks like the work of a wild animal."

PART THREE

HOWLS

Chapter 17

OUT OF THE BAND

"**W**hy did Aunt Margaret lie to me, Dr. Moore?" Danielle asked the next day. "Why didn't she tell me the truth?"

"She lied to protect you, Danielle," he explained gently. "She kept a painful truth from you because she didn't want to hurt you any more than you'd been hurt."

"I—I'm just so upset," Danielle confessed. "Upset and confused. All these years, I—I thought I could trust my aunt."

"You can—" Dr. Moore started.

But Danielle cut him off. "She didn't have to tell me about the horrible way Mom and Dad died five minutes after it happened. But she could have told me later. She *should* have told me later."

Dr. Moore leaned forward in his chair. "I had a long talk with your aunt yesterday—"

"I know that," Danielle interrupted. "I picked up the phone to make a call and heard her talking to you. Why didn't you tell me that the two of you have been discussing me all this time?"

The doctor smiled and shook his head. "Because we haven't," he replied. "Danielle, you can trust your aunt. Believe me. She was very worried about you yesterday, so she called me—for the first time since I've been seeing you."

Yesterday, Danielle thought, gripping the arms of the chair. Until yesterday, she had believed that her parents died in a car accident. Danielle was right about one thing—they'd been torn to pieces. But not on rocks, the way she'd imagined.

They'd been torn apart by animals.

Danielle shuddered. "Aunt Margaret called you because she was worried," she told Dr. Moore. "And I heard you say you were worried, too. I have to know, Doctor—are things worse than I thought?"

"I won't lie to you, Danielle," Dr. Moore replied softly. "I'm concerned, yes."

Danielle's heart sank. She *was* getting worse.

"These fantasies you have are normal, as I've told you," the doctor continued. "But the more you worry, the longer it will take for them to disappear. That's what concerns me."

"You mean I'm making myself worse?" Danielle asked.

"No, you must not blame yourself," the doctor said quickly. "Blame me. I'm the one who's supposed to ease your fears, and I haven't been successful. Yet," he added with a smile.

Danielle couldn't smile back.

Dr. Moore stood up and sat on the edge of his desk. "Let's get to work, Danielle. I want you to put everything out of your mind and concentrate on the numbers."

Starting at one hundred, Danielle slowly began counting backward. She usually felt herself relaxing by the time she reached ninety.

As if from a distance, she heard the doctor say, "Are you feeling all right, Danielle? Are you calmer now?"

"Yes," she murmured.

"Good. Then tell me what you see."

Danielle tensed up again as an image appeared in her mind. "Dee!" she exclaimed. "I'm with Dee!"

"How do you feel about that?" the doctor asked.

"Angry. Scared. She hates me."

"Why does she hate you?"

"Jealous," Danielle replied. "She's jealous about my singing. And about Kit. She wants Kit for herself."

Danielle's breath started coming faster.

"What's happening now?" the doctor asked.

"I'm running," Danielle replied, breathing rapidly.

"Running from Dee?"

She shook her head. "No, we're running on a track. Jogging together." Danielle frowned. "Except Dee's not jogging. She's racing. And—"

"And?"

Danielle panted. "And I'm running after her! I want to catch her. I am! I'm catching up to her!"

"Do you pass her?" Dr. Moore asked.

"No! No, she grabs me!" Danielle cried. "She's furious. She wants to win. She'll kill me to stop me from beating her."

Danielle raised her hands. The fingers curved into claws. "But Dee can't kill me. I won't let her. I'll kill her first!"

Every muscle in Danielle's body tensed. Her breathing came faster than ever. "We're fighting now. Rolling in the dirt. She's strong, but I'm stronger!"

A low groan escaped Danielle's throat. "She's tearing at my hair, but I've got my hands around her neck! I'm going to—"

As if from a distance, Danielle heard the doctor snap his fingers. Once, twice.

She felt her arms and legs start to relax as the fantasy fight with Dee began to fade. She slumped in the chair, breathing easier.

"How do you feel?" the doctor asked.

"I—I don't know," she stammered. "I'm sorry. It didn't really help, Doctor. I just don't know what to do. I've been thinking about quitting the band."

The doctor shook his head. "I can't stop you, of course. But I strongly believe that the band is the best thing for you, Danielle. It gives you a purpose, something to work for."

"Yeah, that's true," Danielle agreed. "Without it, I'd probably just hang out in my room."

"What a waste of talent that would be." Dr. Moore smiled. "You'll be okay, Danielle. You really will. But you and I must keep talking."

Danielle nodded, then stood up as the doctor glanced at the clock on his desk. Her time was up. She wished she didn't have to leave. She felt safe here.

"Is your friend waiting for you outside?" the doctor asked as Danielle walked to the door.

"Yes. Caroline," Danielle told him. "We're going shopping."

"Ah. Spending money is very good therapy, I've heard," the doctor teased.

Danielle forced a smile and said goodbye. The minute she pulled the door shut, she felt tense again.

Get a grip, she told herself. You can't hide out in Dr. Moore's office for the rest of your life.

"Okay, Caroline, I'm—" Danielle stopped and looked around the waiting room. Where was Caroline?

"Excuse me," Danielle said to Mrs. Wilkins, the receptionist. "I had a friend waiting for me—long blond hair, jeans, and a red tank top. Did you see her?"

Mrs. Wilkins hands hovered above her computer keyboard. "I saw her come in with you. But I'm afraid I've been so busy I didn't see her leave."

Caroline probably got bored with the magazines in here, Danielle thought, pushing open the door. She must have decided to wait outside.

Danielle hurried across the small gravel parking lot to Caroline's car. Empty.

"Caroline?" she called, glancing around. "I'm finished! We can go now!"

She heard footsteps crunching on the gravel and turned around. "Caroline?"

No.

Dee strode toward Danielle, her amber eyes blazing.

"What are you doing here?" Danielle asked. "Where's Caroline?"

Dee kept coming. "I want you out of the band, Danielle. Are you listening this time? I want you out!"

Chapter 18

THE KILLER

"What are you raving about now? Where's Caroline?" Danielle demanded.

Dee stopped. "She had to leave."

"Leave?" Danielle pointed to Caroline's car. "So what's this doing here? She didn't have to leave, Dee. I don't believe you. Where is she?"

"It doesn't matter." Dee stepped up to Danielle. "I want to talk to you."

Great, Danielle thought bitterly. Just what I need. "I haven't got time. Besides—"

"Listen to me!" Dee snapped. "Time is exactly what you won't have—if you don't leave the band!"

Danielle leaned back against Caroline's car and crossed her arms. "Look, Dee, I'm not quitting the band—no matter how much you want me to. I'm sorry you aren't the only lead singer anymore. And I'm sorry you're jealous about Kit and me. I really am. But the doctor thinks the band is the best thing for me, and—"

"Leave it!" Dee shouted. "I'm warning you—"

Danielle straightened up, her hands clenched into fists. Rage swept through her like burning fire.

What's happening to me? she wondered. I—I feel so out of control!

With a savage snarl, she dived at Dee. Her fingers curled into claws. She aimed them straight for Dee's throat.

With an angry shriek Dee fought back. She grabbed Danielle's hair and twisted it in her hands.

Danielle cried out in pain. She jammed one hand under Dee's chin and shoved as hard as she could. Dee gasped. Staggered back.

Danielle leaped at her, knocking Dee to her knees.

Why? Why am I doing this? What's wrong with me?

Snarling, she wrestled Dee to the ground. The gravel cut into her elbows, but the pain didn't matter. Winning did. She had to beat Dee!

Dee gasped in pain as the gravel slashed her cheek. Blood!

Danielle could smell it! She could almost taste it. She wanted it. Wanted to feel it in her mouth again. Salty. Thick. Delicious!

She heard herself howl again, howling for the blood like an animal.

An animal.

What was *wrong* with her?

Snarling, she dug her clawlike fingers into Dee's throat.

It's just like my fantasy, Danielle thought.

But it's not a fantasy. It's real.

I'm going to kill her!

Kill her!

Chapter 19

THIRSTY

The smell of blood made her pulse race, her heart pound.

I must taste it!

I must taste it now!

Uttering a howl of attack, Danielle dived for Dee's throat again.

Dee kicked out wildly. Slammed a foot heavily into Danielle's stomach.

"Dee! Danny! Stop it!"

Danielle heard Caroline's startled cries.

Dee leaped on top of her.

I must taste it! Danielle thought, panting loudly.

I must taste the blood!

"Stop!" Caroline screamed. "What are you doing? Are you *crazy*? You're going to kill each other!"

Danielle felt Dee's weight being lifted from her. She scrambled to her feet.

"What's going on?" Caroline demanded, her blue eyes wide with shock and anger. She kept a tight hold on Dee's arm. "What happened?"

"Ask *her!*" Dee shouted breathlessly. "I tried to talk to her, and she came at me like—like I don't know what!"

Like an animal, Danielle thought, panting. She bent over, pressing her hands on her knees, struggling to catch her breath.

Caroline narrowed her eyes at Dee. "You know you're not supposed to get Danny upset! What did you say to her?"

"Nothing," Dee muttered. She yanked her arm free. "Nothing at all. Forget it."

With a last angry glance at Danielle, Dee spun away and ran at full speed out of the parking lot.

When she had vanished from sight, Caroline turned to Danielle. "Wow. That was really horrible! Are you okay?"

Danielle nodded, still breathing hard. "Where—where did you go?"

"I got bored, so I walked over to the river," Caroline explained. She looped her arm around Danielle's shoulder. "Are you sure you're okay? What did Dee say to you?"

"She told me to get out of the band and I—" Danielle took a deep breath. "I jumped on her, Caroline, just as she said!"

"Don't get upset. She made you angry, that's all."

"Angry?" Danielle shook her head. "I was more than angry. I—I wanted to *kill* her!"

"Yeah, well, I don't blame you," Caroline said. "She didn't have any business telling you to leave the band. She's supposed to—" She broke off, biting her lip.

"Supposed to what?"

"She's supposed to do what's best for the band," Caroline finished quickly. "Dee is out of control."

"No, you don't get it," Danielle told her. *"I'm* the one who lost it. I really did want to kill her. And then I saw the blood, and it made me crazy! What's wrong with me, Caroline? It was just so *weird!"*

"Nothing's wrong, except you need to calm down." Caroline replied, keeping her arm around Danielle. "Let's forget about shopping today. Come on, I'll drive you home."

Caroline doesn't want to believe that I'm so totally messed up, Danielle told herself as they drove away. How can she say nothing is wrong?

Danielle glanced across the car at her friend. Caroline frowned and tensely bit her lip. Her hands gripped the steering wheel so tightly the knuckles were white.

She *does* know something is wrong, Danielle thought. And she's afraid.

Maybe she's even afraid of me.

"I've got you now! You're dead meat!"

Danielle ducked down and held her breath.

Silence. Where is he?

Then she heard shuffling footsteps. Loud breathing. She forced herself to keep still.

The breathing got louder. The footsteps closer.

Finally a blond head poked out from behind a large cardboard box.

Danielle grinned and aimed her Super Soaker. "Gotcha!" she shouted and sprayed water onto her brother's chest.

Cliff fell to his knees and tried to catch the stream of water in his mouth. "Help! I'm drowning!"

Danielle laughed, pumped the water gun, and sprayed him again.

After the frightening scene yesterday, it felt good to be out in the backyard playing a game with her little brother.

"How'd you get me?" Cliff asked when Danielle's gun was empty. He pulled up his drenched T-shirt.

"It wasn't exactly hard," Danielle told him as they refilled their water guns from a faucet on the side of the house. "You walk like an elephant, Cliff. And I could hear you breathing a mile away."

"You sound like Aunt Margaret," Cliff complained. "She's always telling me not to breathe through my mouth or else a bug's going to fly in."

"So keep your mouth shut," Danielle advised.

"Yeah, okay." Cliff squirted water on her arm. "Come on, I'll get you this time!"

The two of them ran to opposite ends of Cliff's cardboard fort and took cover.

The cardboard was getting a little soggy, Danielle noticed. "Hey, Cliff!" she called. "Your fort's going to collapse if it gets much wetter. Maybe you ought to find some wood and build another one."

Cliff shouted a reply. Danielle couldn't make out the words.

Now I know where he is, she thought. He falls for that trick every time.

Danielle heard a soft thud.

Grinning, she crept along the length of the fort and turned a corner. Her brother crouched in the dirt. "Gotcha again!" she yelled, aiming the water gun.

"Time out," Cliff protested. "I hurt myself."

Danielle rolled her eyes. "Nice try, Cliff."

"I did! I fell and scraped my arm on one of the boxes. I didn't know cardboard was so sharp." Cliff stood up and held out his arm. "See? It's bleeding."

Danielle moved closer and stared. A small cut, about half an inch long. Bright red blood flowed down the slender arm.

She reached out and took hold of her brother's arm.

"What are you doing?" Cliff cried, trying to pull away.

Danielle tightened her grip.

"That's gross, Danielle! Stop it!"

Cliff's protests buzzed annoyingly in her brain. The words made no sense to her.

The cut filled all her senses. Red. Rich. Pulsing.

Danielle pressed her lips against Cliff's soft skin and hungrily lapped up the blood.

Chapter 20

NIGHT VISITOR

*T*hat night Danielle pulled back the curtains on her bedroom window and gazed out at the backyard.

The moon hovered over the silvery trees, low and full. Its bright light washed over Cliff's sagging cardboard fort.

Danielle turned away from the window.

I can't believe I did that, she thought, raising her hand to her mouth.

I can't believe I drank Cliff's blood.

Think about something else, she ordered herself. A song. Write a new song. Take your mind off what has been happening to you.

Danielle lay down on the bed and propped her legs up on the windowsill. Closing her eyes, she let words and images drift in and out of her mind. She often composed this way, without her guitar. Later, once she had the words in her mind, she put them to music.

After a while the lyrics began to take shape.

> I'm at the window
> howling at the moon,
> crying out my love,
> trying to get through,
> through to you.

> I'm howling, howling,
> howling my love..
> Gotta claw my way back,
> back to you.

Weird, Danielle thought.

Howling my love? Gotta claw my way back?

More than weird. Frightening.

Why am I writing things like this? Stuff about clawing and howling. And killing.

Danielle opened her eyes and sat up. Outside, the moon seemed brighter. She shivered and reached for the curtain.

Her arm stopped in midair.

That shadow on Cliff's fort—was it there before?

Every muscle tensed as Danielle watched the shadow slide across the tattered cardboard and into the cold light of the moon.

Someone lurked in the backyard, staring up at her bedroom window.

Chapter 21

BAD NEWS

Danielle ducked back behind the folds of the curtain. Hidden in the darkness, she struggled to catch her breath.

Then, cautiously, she peered around the curtain again.

A face, pale in the moonlight, tilted toward her window.

Billy's face.

Danielle leaned out the window. "Billy!" she called in a loud whisper. "What are you—wait! I'll come down."

She didn't want to wake her aunt and Cliff. On tiptoe, Danielle made her way downstairs and into the kitchen. She unlocked the back door and eased it open.

Billy crept inside. In the glow of the moonlight that followed him into the room, Danielle could see that he was nervous. His hazel eyes darted around the kitchen, not meeting Danielle's gaze. His hands stayed jammed into the pockets of his faded cutoffs.

Something was wrong.

"What is it?" Danielle asked. "And how come you came sneaking through the yard like that? You really scared me!"

"Sorry. I—" Billy's gaze shifted to the kitchen door. "I started to the front door, but I didn't see any lights and I didn't want to disturb your aunt."

"What's the matter?"

"The matter? Nothing." Billy glanced around the kitchen again. "I—uh—I wanted to make sure you're ready for tomorrow night's show."

Danielle stared at him. Billy wouldn't stake out her backyard at midnight just to make sure she was ready for a performance.

"Billy—"

"The show is here in Shadyside," Billy interrupted quickly. "Makes it a lot easier, right? No packing, no driving, no depressing hotels."

"Right," Danielle agreed. What is his problem? she wondered, studying his face.

"It'll be good to play in front of a hometown audience," he went on. "The manager says we're sold out."

"That's great."

Billy took his hands out of his pockets, put them on

126

his hips, then shoved them back in his pockets again. He stared at his feet.

"Billy, what *is* it?" she demanded. "You're so nervous, you're giving me the creeps."

At last Billy met her gaze.

Danielle jerked away. His eyes! His eyes gleamed with desperation!

Licking his lips, Billy shifted his weight and began inching toward Danielle.

"Danielle, I have—"

"What?" Danielle cried. She took another step back and bumped into a kitchen chair. "What is it? Just tell me!"

Billy kept moving closer to Danielle. "Bad news," he whispered. "I have very bad news."

Chapter 22

DANIELLE GOES HUNTING

"*B*ad news?" Danielle edged around the chair and glanced toward the door leading into the hallway. She suddenly wanted to get away from him. Fast. "What is it?"

"It's Dee," Billy answered.

"Dee?" Danielle stopped moving. "What about Dee?"

"She quit the band."

Danielle stared at him. "She *quit?*"

Billy nodded. "I would have talked her out of it, but she didn't tell me in person. She left me a note."

"Did she say why?"

"Not really," Billy replied. "She wrote that she couldn't handle what was happening."

"She meant me. I know she did," Danielle declared.

"She hated me, hated having to share the lead with me, and—"

"No!" Billy broke in. "It wasn't you, Danielle." He closed the gap between them. "I know it wasn't because of you."

"Then why?" Danielle asked. Secretly she felt relieved. It will be great not to have Dee glaring at me anymore, Danielle thought.

"Why *else* would she leave?" Danielle demanded.

"I—" Billy broke off. He cleared his throat tensely. "Never mind," he told her. "Listen, I better go. Sorry about scaring you before. See you tomorrow at rehearsal."

Billy pushed open the screen door and quickly melted into the shadows of the backyard.

Danielle didn't try to stop him. She shut the inner door and bolted it, glad he was gone.

I'm shaking, Danielle realized. Billy scared me. He acted so strangely. I could see he didn't tell me everything.

What is he hiding?

Back up in her room Danielle closed the curtain and flopped down on her bed. Useless to try to write anything now. She couldn't stop thinking about Billy's visit.

And Dee.

What did Billy want to say about Dee? He was definitely keeping something from her.

Danielle jumped up and began to pace the room. She had the creeps, and being alone made it worse. She needed someone to talk to, to be with.

She picked up the phone next to her bed and listened to the dial tone for a few seconds. Who should she call? Caroline?

No.

Kit.

Kit, with his cool, dark-lashed eyes and his warm smile. Kit, who cared about her.

Kit lived alone in the carriage house of a North Hills estate. It was late. But Danielle didn't care if she woke him up. She needed to talk to him.

Kit answered on the first ring.

"Kit?"

"Danielle," he replied. "Hey, I'm glad you called."

Danielle smiled, happy to hear his voice. "Me too."

"What's up?"

"Nothing. I just—" Danielle paused. "I just wanted to talk to somebody. To you, I mean."

"Well, that's good to hear. But you sound kind of stressed out," Kit said. "Is anything wrong?"

"Not really. Well, maybe," Danielle admitted. "Billy was here. He left about five minutes ago."

Kit's voice rose in surprise. "What was he doing there?"

"I'm not sure," Danielle replied. "He told me about Dee quitting the band."

"Yeah. He called me a couple of hours ago with the news." Now Kit sounded annoyed. "Nice of Dee to give us so much notice, huh?"

"Did Billy tell you about the note she wrote?" Danielle asked.

"Yes, but it didn't make any sense to me." Kit sighed. "Anyway, you said you weren't sure why Billy came to see you. What did you mean?"

"I don't know. He only talked about Dee. But I got the feeling he wanted to say something more." Danielle shivered, remembering the way Billy acted. "He was really uptight, Kit."

"Well, he's got a lot on his mind, especially now that Dee's gone," Kit reminded her. "He's usually pretty cool, but I guess it kind of freaked him out. But don't worry about Billy. He's a good guy."

Is he? Danielle wondered. She used to think so. A great guy, actually. But now she wasn't sure. Something about Billy really troubled her.

"Danielle? You still there?"

"I'm here," she said. "I—I'm just a little messed up."

Kit *tsk-tsked*. "Well, it doesn't sound as if I'm doing much good. Hey, you want me to come over?"

"I'd love it," Danielle replied quickly. "You sure it's not too late?"

"Are you kidding? The later, the better," Kit said. "I'm a night owl, remember?"

"Okay, great!" Danielle thought a second. "But don't come to the door, okay? My aunt's asleep. I'll meet you out front, and we can take a walk."

"Right. Be there in ten minutes."

Eight minutes later Danielle slipped out the front door. She'd changed from her worn T-shirt into a new blue tank top, brushed her hair, and put on a little

131

makeup. She couldn't shake the jitters from Billy's visit. But that didn't mean she couldn't look good for Kit.

He arrived a moment later, killing the engine on his white Mustang and coasting quietly to a stop at the curb.

"You look great," he complimented as he joined her on the sidewalk.

"Thanks." Danielle smiled, feeling calmer with Kit around. "So do you."

Kit glanced down at his ragged jeans and ratty sneakers. He grinned and grabbed her hand. "Come on, let's walk."

They strolled in silence. The moon dipped in and out from behind scattered clouds.

Danielle swallowed hard. For once the cold moonlight wasn't affecting her, wasn't making her feel strange.

Weird, she thought. Usually I'd be shivering. Feeling different. Frightened. But not this time.

It must be Kit, she thought, turning to him. He makes me feel warm and safe.

As if he felt her gaze, Kit smiled at her. "You're not so nervous now," he commented. "Do you want to talk about Billy's visit?"

Danielle shook her head. "I thought I would, but I don't."

"Well, okay," Kit replied softly. "It's just that I thought he upset you, and you wanted to tell me about it."

"I don't," Danielle repeated. "I want to forget it."

Kit let go of her hand and put his arm around her shoulder.

But Danielle shrugged it off. She stared up at the moon and felt a sudden rush of energy. "You know what I want?" she asked. "I want to run. Come on, Kit, let's run!"

Without waiting for him to respond, Danielle took off down Fear Street. Behind her, she heard Kit call her name. But she kept going. Laughing. Running faster.

"Hey, Danielle! Whoa!" Kit shouted from behind her. "You're way ahead. Wait up!"

"Come on and catch me!" Danielle shouted back without slowing down.

Danielle loved the rush of wind in her face and hair. The pounding of her heart. The slap, slap of her sneakers.

Faster! she urged herself. Faster!

"Danielle!" she heard Kit call, far behind her.

But Danielle didn't stop. Didn't *want* to stop!

Why am I doing this? Danielle asked herself. Why am I running like mad in the middle of the night?

She didn't know. She didn't care. She couldn't think. All she could do was run, like a stampeding horse.

Like a wild animal.

"Danielle!" She could barely hear Kit. He'd never catch up.

The wind shifted. Danielle sniffed. Her eyes narrowed and she stopped. She stood still, listening.

Something close by. An animal. Something small.

She could hear its tiny heart racing with fear. She could smell it.

There, in the side yard of that house!

A rabbit. A small, plump rabbit.

Danielle's mouth watered. With one snap of her teeth she'd be able to taste the rabbit's blood. As silently as she could, she leaped over a low hedge and bounded across the yard.

The rabbit stood frozen for a split second, then darted away.

Danielle lowered her head, urged her legs forward. I can catch him! she thought. I know I can!

I can taste the blood already!

Chapter 23

A SURPRISE IN THE TRUNK

"Hey, whoa!" Billy's sharp voice cut through the chatter like a knife. "In case you forgot, we've got a show tonight. You want to try rehearsing instead of standing around shooting the breeze?"

Mary Beth frowned. "We've been rehearsing, Billy. Now we're on a break. Lighten up."

"Rehearsing? Is that what it was?" he shot back. "Could have fooled me. Maybe if you try a little harder, we might be good enough to play for birthday parties!"

Billy made a big deal out of checking his watch. "Five minutes!" he called loudly as he strode away from the stage.

"Wow," Caroline muttered to Danielle. "What's his problem?"

Danielle shook her head. Whatever had bothered Billy last night was still troubling him. But she didn't know what it was.

"Well, I wish he'd cool it," Mary Beth grumbled. "Tonight's supposed to be fun—Bad Moonlight comes home to Shadyside and all that. And he's ruining it with his attitude."

Mary Beth was right, Danielle thought. They were all looking forward to playing in Shadyside. Especially at Red Heat, the most popular teen dance club in town.

Tonight's show was sold out. Red Heat had been a huge warehouse, so "Sold Out" meant an audience of more than two hundred people.

Everybody in the band had been really pumped when they arrived at the club to rehearse. But Billy's sour mood had quickly brought them down.

What was wrong with him?

A husky voice broke into Danielle's thoughts. "Hey, Danielle, please tell me that Billy isn't always like this."

Shawna Davidson, the singer replacing Dee, stepped over to Danielle, brushing out her straight black hair. She was a friend of Kit's. He had called her early this morning. She'd jumped at the chance to be part of Bad Moonlight.

Tall and slender, Shawna was easygoing, with sparkling brown eyes and a good sense of humor. Danielle could tell she was surprised by the manager's mood.

"The first run-through sounded pretty good to me,"

Shawna continued. "But I'm not about to argue with Billy, not on my first day with the band."

"Billy's not always like this," Danielle assured her. "I don't know what's wrong, Shawna. But I'm pretty sure it doesn't have anything to do with the way we sounded."

Shawna glanced at her watch. "Three minutes left. Guess I'd better get ready."

Danielle turned from Shawna and bumped into Kit, who was kneeling next to one of the amplifiers.

"Good. Two extra hands." Kit smiled at her. "You want to hold this cable for me?"

"Sure." Danielle held the fat cable while Kit wrapped black electrical tape around it. When his long fingers brushed hers, she drew back.

Kit glanced up. "Was it something I said?" he asked.

"Excuse me?"

He cut the tape and stood up. "Well, you jumped just now when I touched your hand. And last night, the way you ran away from me, I thought maybe I'd said something or done something to turn you off."

"No! Nothing," Danielle told him. "And I wasn't running away from you, Kit. I was just . . . running."

Funny. She remembered running. But she didn't remember where. Or why.

Danielle uttered a nervous laugh. "Guess I was a little jumpy just now because of Billy," she explained to Kit. "He's acting so strange."

"Yeah." Kit frowned. "I'd sure like to know why."

So would I, Danielle thought. Something to do with Dee, I'll bet. He must be furious because she quit so suddenly.

"Okay, kiddies!" Billy shouted, striding quickly toward the stage. "Recess is over. Time to work!"

Picking up their instruments, the members of the band quickly took their places.

Danielle had changed the lyrics of the song she'd written the night before. This morning she'd worked out the music. She played the opening notes, then began to sing.

> "I'm at the window
> staring at the moon,
> crying out my love,
> trying to get through,
> through to you."

On the refrain, Shawna joined in.

> "I'm crying, crying
> crying my love
> Gotta find my way back,
> back to you."

Their voices blended well—Danielle's high and clear, Shawna's low and throaty.

Danielle was happy with it. But Mary Beth thought it sounded too tame. "It needs something," she insisted.

Danielle laughed. "You should have heard the first lyrics. Instead of 'staring' at the moon, it was 'howling.' And it wasn't "gotta find my way back,' it was 'gotta claw my way back.'"

Mary Beth's green eyes lit up. "That's more like it," she declared. "Let's try it."

The old lyrics still made Danielle uncomfortable. But when they finished the song, Caroline and Mary Beth gave her a thumbs-up.

Danielle tried to shrug off the uneasy feeling.

When they finished that song, they ran through some others, and ended with "Bad Moonlight."

"All right!" Caroline cried when the session was over. "Shadyside is going to rock tonight!"

"Nice work, Shawna," Mary Beth told the new singer. "We're going to be better than ever now."

Billy didn't comment on the band's performance. "Showtime is at nine," he announced. "Everybody be here at eight."

Two and a half hours. Danielle planned to go home, shower, and eat. Maybe catch a short nap.

But first she wanted to talk to Billy, find out what was troubling him.

She caught up to him as he crossed the dance floor to the entrance. "Billy?"

He stopped and turned, obviously annoyed.

Danielle gulped in a deep breath. "I know you've got a lot on your mind, but—Billy, what's the matter?" she burst out. "You're so *angry!* And last night you were all nervous and jumpy."

Billy stared at her, his eyes wide in the red and blue lights of the converted warehouse.

Danielle watched him lick his lips and swallow hard.

He didn't reply. Didn't say a word to her.

Instead, he turned away and hurried out the door.

Danielle arrived back at Red Heat a few minutes before eight. Billy leaned close to Kit on the stage, talking intensely. Caroline and Mary Beth rehearsed their intro to one of the songs.

"Yo!" Danielle called, crossing the big dance floor. "I thought I'd be early, but you guys beat me here."

Kit smiled. So did Mary Beth and Caroline.

Billy glanced at her, then turned away. "Anybody seen Shawna yet?" he asked.

"I'm here!" The entrance door slammed shut and Shawna hurried toward the stage.

"Good," Billy said. "Caroline and Mary Beth wanted to work on something with you."

"Sure." Shawna caught her breath. "My bass is upstairs. I'll go get it."

"I'll get it," Danielle offered. She held up her red dress, covered in plastic. "I've got to put this up there anyway."

"Thanks. It's in the big trunk," Shawna said.

"Be right back." Danielle crossed to the circular metal staircase that led up to the loft.

A couple of dressing rooms were crammed into the low-ceilinged area above the main floor of the warehouse. The rest of the space held extra lights, cables, and other equipment.

Danielle reached the top and flipped on the overhead lights.

She hung her dress on a garment rack in the first dressing room, then went to get Shawna's guitar.

The big trunk, Shawna had instructed her.

Glancing around the shadowy storage area, Danielle discovered three big trunks. Two of them were shoved back against the wall and covered with dust.

Must be the first one, she decided. She examined it. It was a tall, black, upright trunk with three heavy metal clasps.

Danielle started to pry the clasps open.

Wow. It is boiling hot up here, she thought. She wiped her hand across her forehead, brushing away beads of perspiration.

The trunk had been jammed between some cardboard boxes and a stack of folding metal chairs. Danielle grasped the trunk handle and struggled to slide it out.

It didn't budge.

What did Shawna have in here with her bass? A ton of bricks?

The cardboard boxes were loaded with colored gels for the spotlights. Danielle shoved them out of the way.

Then, leaning over the trunk, she pulled open the lid.

And peered inside.

"Noooooo!" She let out a low cry.

Dee's body tumbled out.

Slashed to pieces.

Chapter 24

BILLY KNOWS

Dee's body toppled onto Danielle's shoes.

Danielle staggered back. She opened her mouth to scream, but no sound came out.

Dee's T-shirt and jeans were blood soaked and cut to pieces. Deep, long scratches ran down her arms. Scratches covered her neck as if an animal had clawed at her throat.

Raising both hands to her face, Danielle backed away, crashing into a microphone stand. It fell with a loud clang.

She barely heard it.

Her heart hammered. A loud roar filled her ears. She squeezed her eyes shut, then forced them open again.

As Danielle stared down in horror, she pictured

herself in that frightening fantasy, running with Dee on the track. Running after her.

Attacking her.

Once again, Danielle saw the real fight they'd had, in the parking lot outside Dr. Moore's.

Snarling and wrestling in the gravel. Going for Dee's throat.

She had wanted to kill Dee. Wanted to tear Dee to pieces.

And now Dee lay at her feet. Torn to pieces, as in Danielle's violent fantasy.

Clawed and scratched to death. As Joey had been.

Dee and Joey.

Did I do this? Did I murder Dee?

The terrifying question burst into Danielle's mind.

She shook her head hard. Of *course* I didn't murder them. Of *course* I'm not a murderer.

But she couldn't remember what had happened that night in the park with Joey.

And Dee?

Danielle couldn't remember. Couldn't remember.

Dr. Moore had assured her she wouldn't act out her violent fantasies. But what if he was wrong?

A violent shudder ripped through Danielle. Get out! she urged herself. Get out of here—now!

Danielle tripped over the fallen light pole and landed heavily on the floor. Pain shot through her knee, but she ignored it. Gasping for breath, she scrambled to her feet and raced down the narrow corridor.

Someone waited at the top of the stairs.

"Billy!" Danielle staggered to a stop.

He watched her, not speaking.

She stared into his eyes, her mind racing. Billy acted so nervous last night when he told her about Dee quitting the band. So nervous, he frightened her.

He was hiding something.

Was he hiding Dee's murder?

Did Billy know that Dee was dead when he came to visit Danielle?

Was that why he acted so strangely?

Did Billy murder Dee? Why? Why would Billy murder Dee?

Billy shifted his weight and narrowed his eyes at Danielle.

He knows, Danielle realized. He knows that I discovered Dee's body.

I have to get away. Have to get help.

"Get out of my way!" she screamed at him.

Billy didn't move. He blocked her way to the stairs.

"Let me out!" she shrieked in panic. "Let me out of here!"

"No, Danielle." Billy reached toward her. "I'm sorry. I can't let you go now."

Chapter 25

A HOWL IN THE WOODS

Danielle felt a wave of panic sweep over her.

What can I do? What?

Run back, hide behind something in the storage area? No, I'll be trapped. Cornered.

She turned back to Billy. Anger quickly replaced her fear.

He can't stop me! I won't let him.

"Danielle."

"No!" With a roar Danielle charged at Billy. He stretched his hands out, ready to grab her. She crashed into him at full speed.

He grabbed her arm. The fingers tightened, dug in.

"No!" Danielle swung her fist at him, slamming it into the side of his head.

Billy gasped. His fingers loosened.

With a wild cry Danielle wrenched her arm free, shoved him away, and raced for the stairs.

Halfway down, one of her sandals caught on a metal rung of the staircase. Danielle screamed and fought to keep her balance. The scream echoed in the vast warehouse.

"Danielle!" she heard Caroline cry. "Look out! You're going to fall!"

Danielle kicked off the loose sandal. Stepped out of the other one.

Behind her, heavy footsteps rang out. Billy came racing after her.

Danielle dived down the stairs.

Get out, she urged herself. Run away! As far away as you can!

She jumped over the last three steps, staggered, and caught her balance. Then she lowered her head and plunged toward the door. She caught a glimpse of Kit's alarmed face, and Shawna's. She heard Caroline and Mary Beth call her name.

She didn't stop. Hands out in front of her, Danielle slammed into the bar on the door and burst outside.

Her car was blocked. She couldn't use it anyway. No keys.

Danielle veered away from the cars, her bare feet slapping against the pavement.

Through the parking lot, into the street. Horns blared at her. Brakes squealed. Drivers shouted.

Danielle ignored them. Above the shouting and honking, she heard voices behind her.

"She's getting away! Stop her!"

Faster, Danielle! she urged herself. Faster!

A full moon hung in the dark sky like a gleaming ball of ice. Danielle felt the light wash over her head and arms. Cold. Dangerous.

She ran harder.

Heart pumping, she leaped across the sidewalk and plunged into a dark wooded area.

The voices behind her faded.

Danielle kept running. Pine needles pricked her feet. Branches whipped across her arms and face and snagged at her hair.

Her side ached and the soles of her feet felt raw from running on the pavement. She slowed down, but she didn't stop.

She didn't dare stop.

A vine tangled in her hair, and Danielle hesitated. She heard a sound ahead of her.

She stopped. Listened hard.

Rippling water.

The river flowed to her left.

She knew these woods. She could cut through them and come out near her house.

Gasping with relief, Danielle felt a surge of new energy. She ripped the vine from her hair and started running again.

Batting branches out of her way, she spotted a glimmer of moonlight up ahead through the thick trees. Almost out of the woods, she told herself.

She turned. No one behind her.

Home, she thought. Got to get home.

It was two or three miles on the other side of the woods. But she could make it now. She knew she could.

Billy knows where I live, she remembered. Will he be waiting there for me? Is that why he didn't chase after me into the woods?

She couldn't think about that now. She just had to get home.

A rustling noise off to the right made her heart jump.

She paused, listening, peering into the thick darkness. Silence. A squirrel or a racoon, she told herself. Keep running.

Danielle reached the edge of the woods. She broke through the final barrier of branches and felt soft, cool dirt under her feet.

Which way is home?

Before she could decide, a figure crashed out of the woods and grabbed her arm.

Danielle let out a shriek of startled horror.

"Danielle! It's okay! It's me!"

Caroline!

Danielle sighed in relief. "Help me, Caroline!" she cried. "You've got to help me—or he'll kill me!"

Scratched and exhausted, Danielle flung herself at Caroline. "I—I can't run any farther. Help me, Caroline, please! He'll kill me! He'll kill me too!"

Caroline wrapped her arms around Danielle and held her tight. "Come on, Danny. Of course I'll help you," she murmured softly.

"I've got to get home!" Danielle choked out. "He—he might hurt Aunt Margaret or Cliff!"

"You'll be okay. Catch your breath," Caroline urged her. "I'll help you get home."

Danielle rested her head on Caroline's shoulder. Gradually her breathing slowed. She stopped trembling.

Moonlight poured down on them. Danielle shivered. "Let's go," she said. "Let's get out of here."

"Catch your breath," Caroline repeated. Her voice sounded different—low and hoarse.

"No. Come on. Hurry!" Danielle pleaded. "We can't waste time."

Caroline didn't respond this time. Her hands felt heavy on Danielle's back. Danielle heard a low, rumbling sound from deep in Caroline's chest.

"Are you okay?" Danielle asked.

What's that smell? Danielle wondered. She sniffed the air. It smelled sour. Like a dog that hadn't been bathed in years.

Danielle shivered. "Caroline?" she whispered.

She spun around—and gasped. "No! No! It can't be!"

Caroline's blue eyes gleamed out at Danielle from a face covered in gray fur. The same bristly gray fur had sprouted over Caroline's arms and legs.

Another rumbling sound rose up from Caroline's chest.

And then her thick, purple lips drew back, revealing

sharp yellow fangs. Fangs that glistened with saliva. Fangs that were meant to tear into flesh and rip it apart.

As the cold moonlight poured down, Caroline tossed back her ugly, fur-covered head and let out a long animal howl.

Chapter 26

WHO CAN SHE TRUST?

The long, wailing cry shattered the quiet of the night. It ended in an ugly animal growl.

Caroline's eyes rolled wildly, catching the silver light of the moon. Thick saliva dripped onto the fur over her chin.

Her purple lips drew back again.

"Caroline!" Danielle cried. "You know me. I'm your friend. Please, Caroline!"

Caroline raised her fur-covered hands. The yellow nails had grown long and curled into ragged claws. Claws that could rip and tear.

Another inhuman growl started again, deep in Caroline's throat. She grabbed Danielle roughly with both claws.

"Caroline!" Danielle shrieked. "It's me—it's Danielle! Caroline, please!"

The blue eyes were all that remained of Caroline. The rest of her had transformed into a grunting, drooling creature.

A wolf?

A werewolf?

Choked with terror, Danielle struggled to pull away. But Caroline held on to her with inhuman strength. Then, over Caroline's shoulder, Danielle glimpsed two lights in the distance.

Headlights, she thought. A car. Somebody to help me.

Danielle shrieked as loud as she could. "Help! Over here! Help!"

An engine roared. The headlights loomed closer.

Caroline uttered an angry snarl and snapped her head around. Her grip loosened.

Danielle tore free and sprinted toward the bouncing headlights.

"Hey!" she shouted, waving her arms above her head. "Over here! Help!"

The lights blinded her for a moment. Then they swung away, and she could see the car. Not a car. A van.

The band's van, with Billy and Mary Beth inside.

The van squealed to a halt. Mary Beth and Billy leaped out and sprinted toward Danielle.

"No! Go back!" she cried. "Go back! We've got to get out of here!"

Billy and Mary Beth didn't seem to hear her. As they left the shadows of the trees, the icy moonlight washed over them.

Their faces writhed. Their eyes glittered in the light, and their lips twisted back, revealing sharp, pointed fangs.

Danielle gaped in horror as fur sprouted on their faces, their arms, their hands.

Werewolves! Danielle realized. Billy, Mary Beth, Caroline—they're all werewolves!

Danielle screamed again and whipped around.

Caroline loped toward her on all fours, thick saliva running from her snarling jaws.

Behind her, Billy and Mary Beth tilted back their wolfish heads and uttered shrill howls.

Nowhere to run! Danielle thought, her heart pounding, the blood throbbing at her temples.

"Get away!" she screamed. "Please! Please—get away from me!"

The three wolves moved in front of her, blocking her escape. Backing her up, snarling and growling.

The sickening sour smell rose up in front of her.

The wolves snapped their jaws. Pushed forward.

Backing her up. Backing her up . . .

Until cold water splashed around her ankles.

Danielle cried out. They had backed her into the narrow river.

What did they plan to do? Drown her? Then tear her to pieces?

Tear her to pieces like Joey? Like Dee?

Her foot came down on a smooth, slippery rock.

She fell. Cold water swirled over her legs.

Whimpering in fear, Danielle scrambled to her feet. She glanced up at the van. Not that far away.

Could she get to it before the three wolves attacked her? Could she beat them to it?

She had to.

Sucking in a deep breath, Danielle plunged out of the water. Stumbling and slipping, she cut across the wet dirt.

Behind her, the snarling stopped.

She glanced back. They weren't chasing her. Had they given up?

She struggled to see. But a heavy curtain of darkness had fallen over the woods. A large cloud covered the moon.

"Danny?" she heard Caroline call. "It's okay now. You don't have to run from us." Caroline's voice had returned to normal.

"She's right, Danielle!" Mary Beth shouted.

"You're safe now," Billy added. "We won't hurt you."

Danielle hesitated. She wanted to trust them.

But she knew she couldn't. The moonlight had transformed them into wolves. The bad moonlight.

It had vanished behind the cloud. And they had returned to their human bodies. But the minute the cloud passed, Danielle knew they'd turn into wolves once again and tear her apart!

"No!" she screamed.

And then a voice rang out behind her. "Danielle!"

She recognized the voice. Relief washed over her.

Kit.

"Kit!" she cried. She plunged through the dirt toward his voice. "Help me!"

"Hurry, Danielle!" Kit shouted, holding out his hand. "I have my car. Hurry!"

"The van is closer!" she cried breathlessly.

"I don't have the key. Come on, Danielle, hurry!"

Danielle tried to run, but her legs suddenly gave way. Her muscles cramped. She couldn't move. "Help me, Kit!"

"Danielle, don't go to him!" she heard Billy shout. "He won't save you. Kit is one of us!"

Danielle froze, unable to move, unable to breathe.

"Nice try, Billy." Kit's voice sounded tight with anger. "Don't listen, Danielle. He's lying. Billy is lying to you."

"Kit won't save you!" Billy repeated desperately. "Come to us, Danielle!"

In her panic Danielle turned from Billy to the others, then back to Billy.

"Billy's the band leader—and he's *their* leader, Danielle!" Kit cried. "Come to me and I'll get you out of here."

Kit inched toward her, still holding his hand out. "Come on, Danielle," he urged.

Billy advanced on her. Caroline and Mary Beth moved beside him, urging her to come to them.

What should I do? Danielle asked herself.

Who can I trust?

Who?

Chapter 27

NO ESCAPE

"*T*rust me, Danielle," Kit whispered.

"Trust him?" Billy barked out a sarcastic laugh. "We're your friends, Danielle. Come to us—please."

Breathing hard, Danielle glanced from one to the other. Billy and Kit glared at each other furiously.

Choose! Danielle ordered herself. You have to choose!

She glanced at Caroline and Mary Beth. They nervously watched the sky.

They're waiting for the cloud to pass by, Danielle thought. Waiting for the moonlight to return and transform them into wolves again.

So they can tear me to pieces.

"Kit!" she cried. She spun away from them and raced toward Kit.

He grabbed her hand. "Let's get out of here. The cloud is rolling away!"

She and Kit lurched toward the woods. Danielle felt a surge of hope. We're going to make it!

As they ran, the trees appeared to light up.

It's the moonlight, Danielle realized. The moonlight is back. I can feel its cold light on my shoulders.

"Don't look back!" Kit ordered.

Danielle heard a long animal howl close behind her.

She stumbled, almost pulling Kit down. He grabbed her around the waist and lifted her to her feet.

"Aaaaaagh!"

The wolf roar startled Danielle. She tilted away in time to see Billy leap onto Kit's back.

Roaring and snapping his powerful jaws, Billy drove Kit to the ground.

"Run, Danielle!" Kit gasped hoarsely. "Get away while you can!"

Billy grunted and snarled as he and Kit rolled over and over in the dirt. Kit fought hard. But he was no match for the powerful wolf.

Danielle's gaze snapped back to Mary Beth and Caroline. They crept closer to her on all fours.

I've got to save Kit, Danielle thought frantically. But I can't fight all three of them. I have to get help.

Have to get to the van.

Kit and Billy groaned and grunted, wrestling in the dirt. The other two wolves advanced on Danielle.

She bent low. Scooped up a handful of wet mud.

The two wolves growled, thick saliva dripping from their open mouths.

Danielle sprang up, heaved the mud at their eyes—and took off for the van.

The van was angled sideways, toward the woods. The driver's door had been left open. A glint of metal caught her eye.

The key! The key dangled in the ignition.

With a cry Danielle dived into the driver's seat, pulled the door shut, and slammed down the lock.

Snarling angrily, Caroline and Mary Beth flung themselves against the side of the van, rocking it violently.

With a trembling hand, Danielle grabbed the key.

Turned it.

The engine groaned, started to catch, and died.

Chapter 28

A SURPRISE AT HOME

*T*he headlights beamed toward the trees.

Was the battery dead?

Trembling in fear, Danielle clicked the lights off and grabbed hold of the key again.

Mary Beth and Caroline hurled themselves at the van again, rocking it under their weight.

Danielle's hand, slick with sweat, slipped off the key.

Mary Beth's wild-eyed wolf face pressed hard against the driver's window. Her claws scrabbled at the glass.

Danielle turned the key. The engine groaned. She stopped, pumped the gas, and turned the key again.

At last! The engine roared to life.

Danielle shifted into reverse and stomped on the

gas. The tires spun in the wet dirt. "Go!" Danielle yelled. The van jerked backward. "Yes!"

Mary Beth clung to the side mirror. Danielle hit the brake and shifted, then hit the gas. As the van jumped forward, Mary Beth toppled off, all four fur-covered paws flailing wildly.

In the rearview mirror Danielle watched the two wolves chasing after the van on all fours, snarling and snapping.

She jammed the pedal to the floor and screamed with relief as the van shot forward, leaving the animals behind.

"I made it!" Danielle cried aloud.

But what about Kit?

Please, Kit—please. Find a way to stay alive till I get back.

Guiding the van over the bumpy wooden bridge that led to the street, Danielle took a deep breath and tried to think clearly.

Billy is the leader. Does that mean he killed Joey and Dee?

Why?

She suddenly remembered the animal howls she had heard from her hotel window. Wolf howls. My so-called friends. Howling at the moon.

Danielle remembered her own fingernails lengthening and curling into claws.

She remembered lapping up Cliff's blood. Her furious desire to kill Dee.

Were they trying to turn me into a werewolf too? she asked herself with a shudder.

But it didn't work, she assured herself.

I'm still me. I'm not a wolf.

It didn't work.

Don't think anymore, Danielle instructed herself as the van rocketed down Fear Street, her street. Just get help.

Danielle glanced nervously into the rearview mirror.

Nothing but darkness. No one following.

Her breath caught in her throat. Would she be too late? Would the police find Kit's body, slashed and torn like the others?

"Hang on, Kit!" she murmured.

At last her house came into view. Danielle shoved the driver's door open even before the van bumped onto the curb.

The breath rasped in her throat as she raced up the sidewalk. She stumbled on the wooden front steps. A splinter cut into the palm of her hand. She ignored the pain and scrambled up.

The front door was locked.

"Aunt Margaret!" she cried, pounding with her fist. "Aunt Margaret, open the door! Hurry!"

Silence.

She pounded again, harder this time. "Aunt Margaret! It's me, Danielle! Hurry and open the door!"

Off in the distance an animal howled. A dog?

Or a wolf?

"Aunt Margaret! Cliff!" She hammered at the door. "Hurry!"

She started to run around to the back when she

heard footsteps in the front hall. The porch light snapped on and the lock clicked.

The door swung open. Danielle burst inside and fell against her aunt.

Aunt Margaret wore a light blue summer robe. Her red hair stuck up in spikes, and her eyes were pouchy from sleep.

"Danielle? What's wrong?" she demanded.

Danielle raised her head. "There isn't time to explain. Quick, we have to call the police!"

She started toward the kitchen, but her aunt kept hold of her arm.

"Call the police?" Aunt Margaret asked. "Why? Did something happen at the concert? You look as if you've been in a fight, Danielle!"

"I have!"

"And you're hurt," Aunt Margaret continued. "Come with me to the bathroom. Let's clean those cuts and scratches."

"No!" Danielle cried frantically. "I'm fine. It's Kit who needs help! They're going to kill him!"

"Huh? Kill *who?* Danielle, calm down and tell me!"

"Billy! And Mary Beth and Caroline!" Danielle gasped out. "They're all werewolves!"

Aunt Margaret's eyes grew wide.

"They tried to kill me too, but I got away. But they've got Kit—and they're going to kill him!"

Tugging her arm loose, Danielle ran down the hall and into the dark kitchen. She knocked into a kitchen chair, flung it aside, and grabbed the telephone.

The kitchen light flashed on.

"Danielle," Aunt Margaret said firmly.

Danielle ignored her. She knew her aunt didn't believe her wild story. She'd make her believe later. She started to punch 911.

Aunt Margaret reached out and broke the connection.

"What are you *doing?*" Danielle shouted. "Aunt Margaret, I know it sounds crazy, but it's true. They're werewolves and they're trying to kill Kit—right now!"

Desperately Danielle tried to peel her aunt's fingers from the phone. "Why are you doing this? Don't you believe me? Do you think I'm crazy?"

Aunt Margaret shook her head. "No, dear, I don't think you're crazy at all. In fact I know you're not."

"Then why—?"

"I'm sorry, Danielle, but you can't call the police. I can't let you." A strange smile spread over Aunt Margaret's face. "You have to go back to the others, dear. We've all worked too hard. You can't spoil our plans for you now."

Chapter 29

BIG PLANS FOR DANIELLE

I didn't hear right, Danielle told herself.

Aunt Margaret didn't say that.

But what *did* she say?

Gently Aunt Margaret took the phone from Danielle's hand and hung it up.

"You must go back to them, Danielle," Aunt Margaret repeated. "They won't let you escape. They'll kill you first."

No, Danielle thought. She can't be saying that. This is one of my fantasies. If I just wait, it'll be over.

She felt Aunt Margaret's arm on her shoulder. She stiffened.

"Danielle!" Aunt Margaret sounded hurt. "Don't be afraid of me. Come sit at the table and let me fix you some tea."

Danielle shook her head and shrugged her aunt's hand off her shoulder. "I have to get help for Kit!"

Aunt Margaret sighed. "You can't, dear. Please listen to me. I can't let you ruin our plan, Danielle. We've all been working on it for so long."

Danielle gazed around the kitchen. The clock ticked. The refrigerator hummed. The plants swayed gently in the breeze from the window.

Face it. Everything is all real, Danielle told herself. It's all really happening.

And . . . and . . . Aunt Margaret is one of *them!*

Her eyes moved back to her aunt's face. She swallowed. "You're my aunt!" she whispered hoarsely. "How could you help them?"

Aunt Margaret slowly shook her head. "I'm not your aunt, Danielle."

"Huh? What do you mean?" Danielle shrieked. "I've known you all my life! Of course you're my aunt!"

"You hadn't seen your real aunt since you were a tiny child," Aunt Margaret reminded her.

"But—but—" Danielle sputtered.

"I took her place," the woman revealed.

"But what happened to my real aunt?" Danielle demanded.

The woman brushed back her red hair and sighed again. "You don't have to know that, Danielle. The less you know, the easier it'll be for you to—"

"Tell me!" Danielle demanded.

"Your real aunt is dead," Aunt Margaret replied

bluntly. "Just like your parents. All three of them died the same way."

"What are you talking about? My aunt wasn't with Mom and Dad when they had that car accident!"

"No, of course she wasn't," Aunt Margaret agreed. "But they got her, the same way they got your parents."

"The same way they got—" Danielle stopped, horrified.

The newspaper story! Her parents had been torn to pieces by unknown animals. No wonder she couldn't stop thinking about them. Somehow, all along, she'd known that the accident story was a lie.

And the same animals that killed her parents killed her aunt.

Werewolves.

The werewolves had killed them.

Aunt Margaret continued her explanation. "It was all part of the plan," she told Danielle. "They had to get your relatives out of the way so I could care for you. So I could get you ready."

"Ready for what?"

"Ready for your husband!" Aunt Margaret leaned close to Danielle. Her steely blue eyes gleamed with excitement. "You've fought it hard, but you can't win," she whispered. "You'll never win. And you're almost ready. Almost ready to become his bride!"

"Whose bride?" Danielle cried. "What are you talking about?"

"A werewolf's bride." Aunt Margaret smiled triumphantly. "Our master. He needs a wife, Danielle, and he chose you."

Billy! Danielle thought as a chill of horror swept down her body. They expect me to marry that *creature*.

Danielle crept backward, but Aunt Margaret shot out a hand and grabbed her tightly around the arm. She was a small woman, but her grip was powerful.

"Let go of me!" Danielle demanded. "I won't be part of your sick plan. Let go of me!"

"It's too late!" Aunt Margaret whispered. "Years too late."

Danielle glanced around the room. How can I get out of here? How can I escape from her?

"Don't try anything," Aunt Margaret warned. "It's useless, Danielle. I won't let you go. I won't let you spoil everything."

Danielle jerked her arm violently.

"Stop it!" Aunt Margaret insisted sharply. "You're just making it harder on yourself."

"Hey, what's going on?" a shrill voice demanded.

"Cliff!" Danielle cried. Her little brother stood in the kitchen doorway in his Power Rangers pajamas, blinking at them sleepily.

"What's happening?" Cliff asked with a huge yawn. "I heard all this shouting and stuff."

"It's nothing, Cliff," Aunt Margaret told him quickly. "Go back to bed."

Cliff eyed them suspiciously. "You guys having a fight or something?"

"No!" Aunt Margaret snapped. "Now go back to bed!"

Cliff frowned. "Okay, okay. All I asked was—"

"Listen to me, Cliff!" Danielle interrupted quickly. "Run upstairs and call the police! Call 911."

"The police?" Cliff's eyes widened. "Hey, were we robbed or something?"

Aunt Margaret laughed harshly. "Your sister is trying to trick you, Cliff. You know how she likes to tease."

"No!" Danielle shouted. "This isn't a joke, Cliff. Please, get the police!"

Cliff hesitated. His gaze moved back and forth between his aunt and his sister.

"Cliff, do as I say and get back to bed," Aunt Margaret ordered.

She moved toward him, and her grip on Danielle's arm loosened. With a cry Danielle pulled free and shoved the woman away. The woman staggered, crashed into Cliff, and the two of them fell to the floor.

Ignoring their cries, Danielle dived to the back door, twisted the lock, and yanked it open.

Billy stood outside.

His eyes burned angrily into hers. "Where do you think you're going?" he asked.

Chapter 30

HELP

"Where do you think you're going?" Billy repeated.

"As far away from you as I can get!" Danielle screamed.

Before Billy could react, she thrust out both arms and shoved him down the back steps.

He cried out in surprise. Grabbed for her.

But she leaped over him. She landed hard on her hands and knees, scrambled to her feet, and raced around the corner of the house.

"Stop her!" she heard Aunt Margaret shout from inside the kitchen. Then she heard Cliff's frightened cries.

Would Aunt Margaret hurt Cliff?

No, Danielle told herself. The werewolves aren't after Cliff, she told herself. They want a bride for Billy.

A bride for the werewolf.

Heavy footsteps pounded the ground behind her. Billy!

With a furious burst of energy, Danielle tore through the front yard and jumped into the van.

Her fingers felt thick and clumsy as she dragged the key out of the pocket of her shorts.

It slipped out of her hand. She ducked down and searched the grimy van floor.

Billy threw himself at the van. "Danielle!" he shouted. "Don't run from me!"

She found the key and jammed it into the ignition.

Billy clawed at the driver's window. "Danielle, open the door!" he yelled. "Don't run. You can't escape. You can't win!"

Oh, yes I can! Danielle thought angrily. She pumped the gas and turned the key.

Billy's fingers scrabbled at the window.

"Get away!" Danielle screamed.

The engine roared. She slid the van in gear and peeled away from the curb. In the rearview mirror she watched Billy chasing after her.

Danielle floored the gas pedal and tore down Fear Street. The van swung wildly, and the tires squealed as she steered it around the corner and onto the Mill Road.

Billy was no longer in sight.

I'm safe, she thought. At least for now.

Danielle let up slightly on the gas. She needed to think.

Where can I go? Who will help me?

I could go to the police station. But if they don't believe me, they'll take me home to Aunt Margaret. I'd never escape again.

Who can I trust? Who will help me?

As she sped north on the Mill Road, a face flashed into her mind.

Dr. Moore.

He said she could call him any time, day or night, if she needed help.

Well, she really needed help now.

Danielle wheeled the van around and roared toward Shadyside's business district. The stores and offices stood empty and dark.

Moonlight washed over the darkened buildings.

The bad moonlight.

It changed Billy and the others into wolves, Danielle knew. And it almost made me one of them.

But how?

She had been outside under the moon hundreds of times in her life. And she had never felt strange or violent.

Until she joined the band.

Billy must have some kind of special power, Danielle decided.

The street suddenly darkened. Glancing up through the windshield, Danielle watched another bank of clouds rolling across the sky toward town.

Good, she thought. Maybe the clouds will block out the moon until Dr. Moore and I figure out what to do.

Dr. Moore's big Victorian house came into view.

Be home. Please be home, Danielle prayed desperately.

She brought the van to a screeching halt and jumped to the ground. Gravel dug painfully into her bare feet as she ran across the parking area.

"Dr. Moore!" Danielle pounded on the door with both fists. "Please, it's an emergency! I need help. I'm in danger! Open up!"

The old house remained silent and dark.

Danielle fumbled for the doorbell and jabbed her finger against it over and over. She heard it buzzing inside. She kept one hand on the button and pounded on the door with the other.

At last the outside light flashed on. A chain rattled, a lock clicked, and the door swung open.

Dr. Moore stared out at her, blinking with surprise. He wore rumpled pants and a loose-fitting sweatshirt. His fringe of gray hair lay matted to his head.

"Thank goodness!" Danielle gasped, pushing her way inside. "I was afraid you were gone!"

"I fell asleep on the couch, reading," Dr. Moore explained, rubbing his hand over his face. "What is it, Danielle? What has happened?"

Danielle slammed the door. "I don't think Billy will figure out that I came here," she said in a frightened whisper. She turned the lock and slid the chain into place. "But I can't be sure, Dr. Moore. He's got some kind of power!"

The doctor's eyes widened in confusion. "What are you saying? Are you being chased?" he asked, studying her face. His expression changed. "You're hurt, Danielle! Your face is scratched and bruised. Come into the office and let me take a better look."

"I'm all right," Danielle insisted as the doctor ushered her into his office. "The scratches don't matter. Please! I'm in danger, and so are you—if he finds out I'm here!"

"Stay calm," Dr. Moore urged softly. "You can explain it all to me in a moment. First, let me make sure all the doors and windows are locked."

She watched him hurry out of the office.

At least I'm safe for now, she thought, breathing a little easier. But what can we do? What can he and I do against a pack of werewolves?

The doctor returned a few seconds later. "Everything's locked," he told her, shutting the door behind him. "And the alarm system is on. No one can get in."

"They'll find a way," Danielle replied. "You don't know them. Even if they don't, we can't stay in here forever. And they'll be waiting for us when we come out!"

"Danielle." Dr. Moore's forehead wrinkled in concern. "Try to calm down and tell me what happened."

"I can't calm down!" Danielle cried, pacing the office again. "You don't understand, Dr. Moore! You don't know!"

"No, I don't," the doctor answered gently. "You have to tell me, Danielle."

174

"They're werewolves!" she burst out. "I know it sounds crazy, but it's true. Billy and Caroline and Mary Beth—they're all werewolves. Aunt Margaret, too, except she isn't my real aunt. She's—"

Dr. Moore held up his hand. "You've lost me. I'm sorry. Please. Take a deep breath, Danielle. Start at the beginning."

Danielle forced herself to stand still. She took a deep, shaky breath, crossed her arms over her chest, and began to talk.

She told him everything, trying to keep it all straight. She kept her voice as calm as she could so he wouldn't think she was crazy.

Dr. Moore listened without moving, without blinking. When she finished her story, he strode to the small refrigerator in the corner and pulled out a carton of orange juice. "Drink some of this," he instructed, handing it to her. "You're in shock."

"No—I'm not!" Danielle declared angrily. "You've *got* to believe me! I'm not making any of this up! I'm not!"

"Did I say you were?" he replied. "You're burning up too much energy too quickly. Your body needs the sugar. Or, if you like, I can give you an injection to help calm you down."

"No!" Danielle grabbed the carton and tilted it to her mouth. "I have to stay alert."

The doctor nodded calmly. "That's fine. I want to help you, Danielle. But won't you at least sit down? You need to rest."

Danielle shook her head. "Billy might figure out

that I came here," she said. "So we need to think of some way to catch them."

"A trap?"

"Yes." Danielle drank some more orange juice. "It'll have to be inside. If they're out, under the moonlight, they'll change into wolves. And then we won't stand a chance."

"Yes, I see."

"You do?" Danielle asked. "Then you . . . believe me?"

The doctor nodded solemnly. "I believe you."

"Thank goodness!" Danielle finished the juice. She felt better. Stronger. "Okay. So, let's figure out how we're going to trap them."

A knock on the door made Danielle drop the juice carton. The orange juice puddled around her feet.

"Dad?" a voice called. "Where is she? Is she in there with you?"

Danielle recognized the voice at once.

Kit!

Danielle's heart raced. Kit was alive!

"Yes, Kit, your bride is waiting for you in here," the doctor answered. He pulled open the office door. "How did you let her get away?"

Chapter 31

NO ESCAPE

Kit stalked into the office. "Thanks, Dad," he said solemnly.

His expression brightened as he turned to Danielle. "Here you are!" he exclaimed.

Danielle could almost feel the blood draining from her face.

I had it all wrong, she realized.

I made the wrong choice.

It's not Billy. It's Kit.

They want me to be Kit's bride.

"I don't understand how you could have let such a thing happen, Kit," Dr. Moore said, shaking his head. "You're very lucky that she came to me, or she might have gotten away."

"Sorry, Dad. It couldn't be helped." Kit grinned at Danielle. "But she's here now. So everything's okay."

"No!" Danielle whispered hoarsely. She backed behind the desk as Kit started for her. "Don't come near me!"

"Danielle, listen—" Kit began.

Dr. Moore cut him off. "Leave her alone for a few moments, Kit," he ordered. "After all, she's had her share of shocks tonight. Give her a chance to calm down."

Kit nodded. "No problem," he murmured. He sat down in the deep armchair in front of the desk.

"How did you get away from Billy and the others?" Danielle cried.

Kit shrugged. "Simple. As soon as you took off in the van, I let the moonlight do its work. Billy and the others are no match for me."

"You're one of them," Danielle said numbly. "All along, you've been one of them." She turned to Dr. Moore. "And you're Kit's father, so you're one of them too."

The doctor nodded gravely.

"But I'm not just one of them, Danielle," Kit told her. He leaned forward in his chair. "I'm the pack leader."

"I thought Billy—"

"Billy!" Kit waved his hand as if swatting away a fly. "Billy does what I tell him to. Know why I made him band manager? To keep you from guessing the truth about me. But he and Caroline and Mary Beth—they are all under my control."

"As you will be soon," Dr. Moore told Danielle quietly.

Danielle shook her head furiously. "You're both crazy! It's not going to happen. You might think you can control me, but I won't let you!"

"You don't have any choice," Kit told her.

"My son is right," Dr. Moore agreed. "But there's no reason to panic. You are already being controlled."

"Huh? What are you talking about?" Danielle cried.

"Your therapy," Kit said. "Your visits with my father."

Danielle stared at the doctor.

"It's really very simple," Dr. Moore told her. "I haven't been treating you at all. While you were hypnotized, I gave you suggestions. Planted ideas in your head that would make you fall under the spell of the moonlight."

"You need moonlight to change," Kit told her. "But it isn't enough. You have to *want* to change, too. At least at first. So Dad gave you the desire."

"Hypnosis is such a wonderful thing." The doctor chuckled. "I even planted your songs in your mind, Danielle!"

The songs, Danielle thought. Weird songs about killing and howling and clawing and dying. Now she understood why she'd been writing that stuff.

"See, Danielle?" Kit said. "The control is already happening. It's been happening for almost three years."

"You're lying!" Danielle shouted. "I didn't even know you three years ago!"

"But I knew you," Kit told her. "Maybe you don't remember. But three years ago you went to a rock concert in the park. A bunch of bands performed."

Danielle did remember that concert. Not because of the music, though. She remembered it because three nights later, her parents died.

"Mine was one of those bands," Kit went on. "Different musicians, but the same roadie—me. When the concert ended, I saw you hanging around, hoping to get autographs. And that's when I knew."

"Knew what?"

"That you would be my bride." Kit's pale blue eyes gleamed.

Wolf eyes, Danielle thought.

Danielle shuddered. How could I have ever thought his eyes were beautiful? she asked herself. They're so cold. So . . . dead.

"Once I had chosen you, I worked out a plan to make you mine," Kit continued. "First, of course, I needed to isolate you. To get you alone."

Isolate. The word hit Danielle like a hammer. She knew what Kit was talking about.

"My parents," she uttered in a voice filled with hate. *"You* killed my parents." Danielle fought back the urge to hurl herself at him. Scratch and kick and bite. Anything to hurt him as much as he'd hurt her.

Kit nodded. "And your aunt. I had to get them all out of the way, or my plan wouldn't work."

"It *isn't* going to work!" Danielle told him hotly. "I

promise you that. You can kill as many people as you—" She stopped, remembering.

As if he could read her mind, Kit nodded again. "You're thinking of Joey and Dee. You're right, Danielle. I killed them too."

Images of their bodies flashed through her mind. Shredded and torn. She blinked the ugly pictures away and stared at Kit. "Why?" she demanded. "They were part of your group. Why did you have to kill them?"

"Joey knew you belonged to me, but he flirted with you anyway." Kit's eyes glared angrily. "I warned him not to come on to you. But he wouldn't stop. I couldn't put up with that. Joey had to go."

"What about Dee? What did she do, forget to bow down to you?" Danielle screamed.

Kit jumped up, clenching his fists.

"Kit," Dr. Moore said. "Don't let yourself get angry. We're too close, son."

"Right." Kit slowly relaxed his hands. He advanced slowly toward the desk.

Danielle trembled.

But Kit passed her and strode to the little refrigerator. He grabbed a bottle of water and took a long swallow. "Dee tried to warn you about me," he told Danielle, as if there hadn't been any interruption. "She betrayed me. She tried to warn you away. Tried to make you leave the band."

Danielle closed her eyes. Dee tried to save me, she suddenly realized. I thought she hated me. But all the time she was trying to warn me.

And Kit killed her for it.

"Don't you understand, Danielle?" Kit asked. "I couldn't let Dee warn you. I worked too hard. I couldn't let her frighten you away and ruin everything."

Danielle shook her head sadly.

Kit sighed. "And then Billy tried to save you too."

"Billy?" Danielle's eyes flew open. "I thought Billy works for you."

"Yes, he's my slave, like Mary Beth and Caroline," Kit agreed. "But it's hard to keep control of a wolfpack a hundred percent of the time. Especially in daylight. And Billy started to get some ideas of his own. Earlier tonight he really wanted to save you. Luckily, you chose to come to me."

"Poor Billy," Dr. Moore murmured.

"Yes, I liked him too," Kit said. "But he'll have to die for trying to save you, Danielle."

"You're sick!" Danielle cried. "What do you have to kill him for? Just let him go!"

Kit's eyes grew colder. "No one betrays me. No one."

Danielle shivered under his icy stare. "You'll have to kill me too."

"Never," Kit whispered. "I would never kill you."

"The bride of a werewolf is completely under his power, Danielle," the doctor told her. "Once you and Kit are wed, you won't *want* to turn against him."

"You'll forget everything but how much you love me," Kit added.

Danielle turned her head away. She couldn't stand

the sight of him. How could I have ever let him touch me? she thought.

Kit sighed again. "I guess I can't expect you to be glad yet," he told her. "But you will. You will, Danielle."

Never, Danielle thought. I'll never be glad, because it's never going to happen!

She had to get out.

Without turning her head or raising her eyes, she glanced quickly around the office.

The doctor stood at the door. Kit near the desk. I'm trapped, she saw.

Or was she?

Behind the desk tall windows opened onto a terrace.

Beyond the terrace stood the yard. Beyond the yard, the river.

Smash the windows, she told herself. Grab the desk chair and smash the windows. Then run for your life.

The chair was one of those heavy leather ones. She wouldn't be able to lift it. But it was on wheels. If she rammed it against the windows, it might do the job.

"It's time," Kit announced. "Come, Father. Perform the ceremony. Marry Danielle and me out in the yard. Under the moonlight."

Kit and his father started toward Danielle.

With a frantic cry she snatched the stapler off the desk and threw it at Kit's face.

He ducked, and it smashed against the wall.

Danielle grabbed the chair.

But before she could send it crashing into the window, Kit leaped forward and grabbed her. He drew his face close to hers. "You can't win," he whispered, his hot breath making her flesh tingle.

Danielle spun around, grabbed hold of his hair, and yanked as hard as she could.

Kit gasped.

Danielle kicked out at him and yanked his hair again.

Then a strong hand clamped down on her shoulders. "You're only making it harder on yourself," Dr. Moore told her. "Get the windows, Kit."

With the doctor holding her, Danielle watched furiously as Kit opened the windows to the terrace.

"Come, Danielle." Kit turned to her, smiling. "Come be my bride. It's time."

I have no choice, Danielle realized to her horror. I cannot escape.

Chapter 32

MOONLIGHT WEDDING

Kit and his father dragged Danielle through the windows and onto the terrace. Danielle didn't make it easy for them. She twisted and squirmed, then went limp and dragged her feet.

But the two men kept pulling her, across the stone terrace and down the steps to the yard.

"Look, Danielle," Kit commanded. "Look at the people who have come to our wedding."

Danielle tossed her head back. Caroline, Mary Beth, Aunt Margaret, and Billy had gathered in the yard.

"Billy!" she cried. "Caroline! Stop them! Help me, please!"

Caroline shifted her weight nervously. She lowered her eyes, avoiding Danielle's gaze.

"Billy, help me!" Danielle pleaded.

Billy stared back at her. The defeated expression on his face made Danielle gasp.

"He's going to kill you, Billy. Did you know that?" she shouted. "Kit's going to kill you because you had the nerve to go against him. Are you just going to stand there?"

"I don't believe you," Billy responded dully. "My master would never do that."

"You see, Danielle?" Kit whispered in her ear. "They are members of my pack. They trust me to do what is right for them."

Danielle glared angrily at the wedding party. Caroline still wouldn't meet her eyes. Mary Beth appeared dull and robotic. Aunt Margaret smiled happily at Dr. Moore.

"You should see yourselves!" Danielle screamed. "You're pathetic! Ridiculous! How can you let Kit control your lives?"

"Insulting them won't work," Dr. Moore told her. "Nothing will work, Danielle."

Danielle glared at him, but she knew he was right. Nothing would work.

She was trapped.

The doctor clapped his hands like a master of ceremonies. "Let us begin," he called.

The group in the yard formed a loose circle around Kit and Danielle.

She had never felt so alone.

Kit took Danielle's hand. "Before my father marries us, I want you to sing, Danielle."

She stared at him, unbelieving. "You've got to be—" Danielle broke off.

Go ahead and sing, she told herself. Anything to buy some time.

Time to think of a way out.

"What song do you want?" she asked Kit.

"'Bad Moonlight.'" Kit laughed softly. "I think of it as our song." He squeezed her hand.

His touch made her stomach tighten.

"Fine," she replied softly. She cleared her throat, took a deep breath, and began to sing in a high, thin voice.

> "Bad moonlight, falling over me,
> Bad moonlight, shining down on me.

Her voice trembled. I can't do this, she thought.

She turned her eyes to Kit and his father. They both watched her. Kit had a smile frozen on his face. Dr. Moore nibbled his lower lip tensely.

"Keep singing, Danielle," the doctor insisted. "Kit, she's wasting time."

"She's just nervous. Right, Danielle?" Kit asked.

Danielle nodded. *Terrified* was more like it. She thought her heart might pound right through her chest.

"She's trying to figure out a way to escape," Dr. Moore said.

Kit shrugged. "Even if she is, it won't do her any good. There *is* no escape. Not now. Relax, Father."

Kit controls him too, Danielle realized.

"Keep singing, Danielle," Kit told her. "Don't worry about how you sound."

Danielle cleared her throat again. Her voice still sounded small and weak.

She coughed. "Some water would help," she murmured to Kit.

Dr. Moore shook his head impatiently. "She doesn't need water, Kit. Make her finish the song so we can get on with this."

Kit glanced up at the sky. Danielle followed his gaze. The clouds she'd seen earlier were still overhead. But they were moving.

The moon would shine down again soon.

"It's almost time," Kit told Danielle. "But I'd really like to have the song at our wedding. Hum it if you have to."

Danielle turned her back on Kit and faced the others.

"Go on!" Kit urged. "Finish the song."

Softly Danielle began to hum the tune. As she did, she moved around in the circle of Kit's wolf pack, staring into each one's eyes.

They don't control their own minds anymore, she realized. Kit does. I'm the only one who can think for myself.

But the song would be over soon, and she still hadn't thought of a way to escape.

Humming softly, Danielle approached Billy and gazed into his eyes.

Do something, Billy! she begged him silently. Don't let this happen!

Billy's lips parted. "I tried to save you, Danielle," he whispered. "But you ran."

Danielle felt a surge of hope. Billy spoke to her! The real Billy, who cared about her.

"I tried," Billy whispered again. "But I can't do any more. You will have to save yourself."

Danielle quickly whispered, "Save *myself*? What can I do?"

"Raise your eyes to the bad moonlight," Billy replied. "Go with it. Let it happen."

"But—I can't!" Danielle protested.

"You can," Billy whispered. "Let the moonlight take you. You will know what to do."

Danielle turned away from him, questions racing through her mind. Was this really the Billy who cared? Or the one who was Kit's slave?

Could she trust him?

Or was his advice a trick?

If it was a trick, she'd be lost. But she was as good as lost now.

Danielle finished the song.

"Good!" Kit exclaimed. "Now we will be married. Father, begin the ceremony."

Kit took Danielle's hand. His touch repulsed her, but she forced herself not to jerk away. I have to keep him off guard, she thought.

Dr. Moore followed and stood facing them.

Danielle glanced at the sky again. The clouds floated apart, spreading away from the moon. The escaping moonlight outlined the clouds in silver.

"Raise your eyes to the bad moonlight," Billy had told her.

What will happen if I take his advice? she wondered.

What will happen?

"Friends," Dr. Moore began solemnly. "Join hands as we witness this marriage, this wonderful union that we've waited for so long."

The small group reached out and held each other's hands.

The circle drew tighter.

Danielle faced Kit. As Dr. Moore spoke, she noticed a glimmer of moonlight touch Kit's dark hair.

Could she trust Billy?

Could she?

Slowly Danielle raised her eyes to the sky. The clouds had drifted away.

The moon floated low overhead.

Danielle shivered in its icy glow, but she didn't turn away. She stared straight up into the bad moonlight.

And waited.

Chapter 33

BAD MOONLIGHT

Seconds passed. Danielle heard Dr. Moore's voice. She felt Kit holding tightly to her hand.

Then she felt her body start to change.

Her skin tingled, then began to itch.

Her throat tightened. She coughed. Her voice escaped in a low rumble.

She felt the hair grow on her hands, over her arms. Thick and bristly.

She curled the fingers on her free hand and felt claws digging into her palms. She felt her face twist, felt her nose and mouth pull forward into a snout, felt her teeth extend as her lips pulled back in an animal snarl.

"When the bad moonlight changes you, you will know what to do."

Billy was right, Danielle thought. I *do* know what to do.

She inched closer to Kit.

A low growl started deep in her belly. It rose up through her entire body until it escaped her mouth as a bellowing roar.

Then Danielle pulled open her powerful jaws and sank her teeth deep into Kit's throat.

She heard Kit's startled howl of pain.

She heard the shocked cries of the others.

She saw the circle break. Saw Aunt Margaret raise her hands to her cheeks in horror. Saw Dr. Moore's eyes go wide, his knees buckle.

Danielle held on.

Held on. Held on.

Dug her wolf teeth deeper into Kit's fleshy throat.

A shrill whistle burst from Kit's open mouth. He whipped his head furiously back and forth.

Danielle staggered. But held on. Held on.

Kit's whistle became a bleat of pain. Blood flowed down his neck.

The whistle became a choked whimper.

He sank to his knees.

Danielle sank with him, grunting, groaning, uttering sharp, breathy growls, her teeth buried in his throat.

She didn't let go until Kit's eyes rolled up in his head, and he sank lifelessly to the grass.

She heard the cries of the others. But turned

her eyes to the moon. To the pale, white moonlight.

The bad moonlight. Sinking once again behind the clouds.

The light fading. Fading . . .

Danielle's body tingled and ached as she returned to human form. She shut her eyes tightly and waited for the painful feeling to stop.

She opened her eyes in time to see Dr. Moore fall to his knees. His entire body began to quiver and shake. Harder. Harder. As if trapped in his own personal earthquake.

His arms flew up as his body shook even harder. And then parts of him began flying off.

His body is shaking apart, Danielle realized, gaping in horror.

Dr. Moore's arms flew off his shoulders. His ears flew away from his quivering head. And then his head flew apart. Danielle covered her mouth as it splattered on the ground.

Danielle spun away. Saw the woman who had been Aunt Margaret shake apart too. Saw Kit's body shake and fly apart. Heads and arms, hands and feet strewn over the grass.

"Ohhhh. Ohhhhh. Ohhhhh no."

Were those sickened moans coming from her own throat?

And then, Billy, Caroline, and Mary Beth came rushing up to surround her.

Billy's eyes glistened with admiration. "You did it, Danielle. You set us free."

193

"You've released us!" Caroline cried happily. She threw her arms around Danielle and hugged her. "Thank you, Danielle. Thank you!"

"Kit used the bad moonlight to hold us prisoner," Mary Beth explained. "We weren't strong enough to break free." Her green eyes burned with gratitude. "Thank you, Danielle. You broke his spell. We've got our lives back now."

They swarmed around Danielle, smothering her in joyful hugs.

After many tears and cheers of celebration, Danielle managed to break away from her happy friends. She ran into the house and called home. Cliff was fine. He didn't know that anything was wrong. He was angry that she'd awakened him.

Danielle felt a strong wave of affection for her brother. They were orphans now. She'd have to fight to keep them together. But she'd faced-off with a werewolf—and won! Now she could face anything.

After telling her brother she'd be home soon, Danielle returned to the others. Caroline and Mary Beth had flopped down on the terrace steps and were gazing up at the sky.

They stared at the moon, as if seeing it for the first time. The white light washed over them, cleansing and pure.

Billy wrapped his arm tenderly around Danielle's shoulders. "We don't have to dread the moonlight anymore," he confided. "Thanks to you."

Danielle leaned against him. "I don't care if I never see the moon again," she said, sighing. "Know what I'm looking forward to?"

"What?" Billy asked.

Danielle grinned up at him. "Some bright sunlight!"

About the Author

"Where do you get your ideas?"

That's the question that R. L. Stine is asked most often. "I don't know where my ideas come from," he says. "But I do know that I have a lot more scary stories in my mind that I can't wait to write."

So far, he has written nearly three dozen mysteries and thrillers for young people, all of them bestsellers.

Bob grew up in Columbus, Ohio. Today he lives in an apartment near Central Park in New York City with his wife, Jane, and fourteen-year-old son, Matt.

THE NIGHTMARES
NEVER END ...
WHEN YOU VISIT

FEAR STREET®

Next ...
FEAR STREET
COLLEGE WEEKEND
(Coming in July 1995)

Tina Rivers can't wait for her first college week-end. She hasn't seen her boyfriend Josh for months. But when she arrives at the train station, Josh's roommate Chris is there to meet her. He tells her Josh went camping and couldn't get back in time.

Tina is disappointed, but Chris shows her around. He knows everything about her, from her favorite foods to her favorite music. It's a little bit creepy.

Is Chris just a nice guy, or is he dangerously obsessed? And what really happened to Josh?

R.L. Stine